Tucker McBride

Doris Gaines Rapp

Huntington, Indiana

Copyright 2019 Doris Gaines Rapp

Daniel's House Publishing   Huntington, Indiana

Huntington, Indiana 46750   website: www.dorisgainesrapp.com
contact: dorisgainesrapp@gmail.com

This book is a work of historic/biographic fiction. Some characters and incidents are products of the author's imagination and are used fictitiously. Conversations were created out of the author's imagination. The timeline of the actual events is compressed.

Cover design is stock imagery from @Dreamstime.com. Put in place by @Debi Lindhorst/The Type Galley. Other images are from the internet
.

Library of Congress Control Number: **2019906293**

ISBN: **ISBN-13: 978-0-9988590-3-3**   (paperback)
ISBN: **ISBN-13: 978-0-9988590-4-0**   (eBook)

Warning

Tucker McBride was an adventurous kid, one who rarely thought before he acted. Learn from Tucker. Do not try Tucker's stunts.

Glossary

For an unfamiliar word with an asterisk (*) beside it, go to the back of the book for a definition or picture.

Table of Contents

Dedication

Dedicated to my dear husband, Bill Rapp, the real Tucker
McBride. You are just as active, just as adventurous as you
were the day I first met you at North Central College in
Naperville, Illinois, so many years ago.
Your stories of family and childhood have entertained
friends and family for many years.
Love you always.

Acknowledgements

Thanks to my writers group, Soli deo Gloria (to God be the
     Glory) for their encouragement, patience, and
     willingness to share their faith in God.
Many thanks to Vicki Borgman for her time and creative
     energy in editing *Tucker McBride*. The many stories
     are of a young boy she heard about all her life, since
     Tucker is actually her dad, Bill Rapp.
I'd like to give a great big thank you to all six of our
     children: Vicki, Donna, Jim, and Vonn. Also, Katy,
     and Mandi, two baby sisters we adopted in our
     middle life.. You all moved with us when you didn't
     want to leave friends. You went without things other
     kids your age had because you were in a parsonage
     family. Your love and presence in our lives, have
     been a blessing to Dad and me.
Debi Lindhorst at the The Type Galley in Warren, Indiana
     can do all of the tech stuff I can't do. Thanks for
     rescuing me, Debi.
A delightful woman named Christmas Tree, was thrilled
     when I asked to use her name as a character in one of
     my novels. Thanks again, Christy.
I send a huge thank you to all of Bill's family and to the
     church family across the street. You made me one of
     yours. Some have moved on to their all-time home
     but I can feel them on the side streets of Dunlap,
     Indiana. They also fill the sanctuary pews with their
     love.

Map of Tucker's Neighborhood

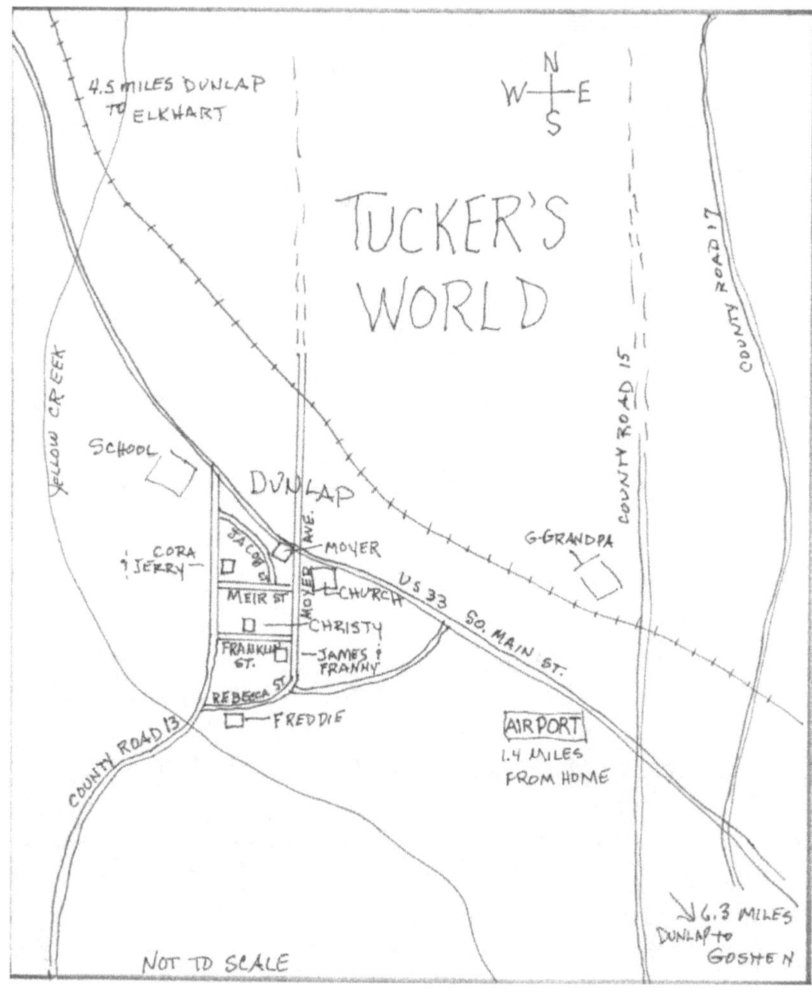

Chapter 1
A High Hideaway

Saturday, June 29, 1946

"Tucker?" The boy heard Gramma Moyer call from the side porch.

"Oh no." He cringed* and ducked his head. Gramma's high pitch on the last syllable meant she was serious. He had to hide … now! Holding his breath, he slid down farther and tried not to fidget, a talent he hadn't mastered yet.

Tucker loved to create his own adventures. Some of the family called him a daredevil. He didn't think he was having fun unless he was scared and charged with hyped up energy at the same time. It was his way of blocking out anything he didn't have a mind to face. Tucker's family collapsed when he was three months old. His mother died during an appendicitis attack. He and his older brother and two sisters went to live with Gramma and Grandpop.

Normally, he would have answered Gramma immediately but not this time. What was a fella to do when he wanted to obey his grandmother but obedience was not in his own best interest? Living with his grandparents, he tried to help Gramma, to make life easier for her. At twelve years old, he helped her with jobs he often didn't know how to do.

Since he couldn't figure out how to get himself out of the jam, he decided to stop thinking about it. He'd pretend he was down in a coal mine or flying over enemy territory to report to headquarters how many troops were advancing on the Allied forces. Now, the war was over, so he decided he was an aerial cameraman for 20th Century Fox. He'd get great shots of Roy Rogers riding across the hills for Republic Pictures.

To satisfy the grumbly spot in his stomach, a possible noisy give-away to his location, he pulled a Baby Ruth candy bar from his pocket, peeled back the corner, and bit off a mouthful of peanuts, caramel, nougat and semi-melted chocolate. He wiped his sticky fingers on his jeans then shoved the other half of the bar back into his pocket. Picking up one of the comic books he had taken into his hiding place, he studied the cover. *Superman would have known what to do. He wouldn't have hid. Hum…wonder if I'm hiding from something?*

Tucker hoped Gramma wouldn't start down the porch steps and find him. He couldn't see her from his vantage point, but he figured Gramma positioned herself in her usual spot, just one shoe out the screen door. Habits of the heart included her pausing to look across Moyer Avenue, the side street running from the highway, past the Dunlap Evangelical Church on the other side. Tucker knew Gramma always looked up at the church and smiled. Her face would soften when she saw the red brick building with the square tower on top for a steeple. It was the place of worship she called, "our church."

Although Tucker's mother had died, his four aunts and uncles and their families went to the church. Now that Tucker and his siblings lived with Gramma and Grandpop, the congregation had grown to a large family church, plus friends and neighbors.

From where Tucker was hiding, he could hear Gramma mumble, "Where is that boy?" He didn't move. He hoped no one would see him. Deep down, he realized being invisible was a silly thought.

Tuck always came when Gramma called. At his age, Tucker knew he didn't want to cause the little lady any anguish. She may have been only four foot ten and a half inches tall, but she had twice the power in every inch than most seventy-five year olds. He didn't want to disobey her. The other foolish notion was that she wouldn't know where he was. All she had to do was step down the porch steps and into the yard.

Tucker remained as quiet as a boy who never stopped moving could. He stretched out on his back, and stared up at the morning sky. The early morning sun hung over the sweet smelling apple trees in the orchard and made Tucker wonder what Gramma was fixing for lunch. *Go back in the house, Gramma,* he begged inside his head. He hoped his thoughts would be strong enough to persuade his grandmother to retreat without revealing the predicament he was in. *How can I get myself out of this mess without Gramma seeing me?*

Tucker turned his red ball cap around hiding the bright bill down his back. Dark brown wavy hair exploded around the edges of the hat. Peering over the side, he watched from his hideaway near the border of the canvas.

From off to the right, he heard the crunch of gravel that lined the edge of the road. Peeking out from where he hid, he saw a woman walking up the street at a fast pace, her lace-up Oxford shoes* with the little heel clicked on the pavement and gritted at the gravel as she moved along. Tucker slapped both hands over his eyes. *Oh no, Mrs. Stuart is here.*

Sneaking another glimpse, Tucker watched with one eye as Adele Stuart hurried along past the rapidly growing corn stalks in the garden. Mrs. Stuart was one of the many neighbors who helped keep track of the super-active, easily distracted boy. In return, Tucker cleaned winter ice off Mrs. Stuart's front walk and raked leaves for old Mr. Jameson. Everyone within a mile or more of his home was Tucker's friend.

Arf, arf, arf. Tucker pulled his knees up into a ball when he heard Tiny burst out past the screen door behind Gramma. *No, no! Not Tiny.* Tucker was afraid the silky terrier would knock his grandmother off the porch with all the little dog's yipping and jumping until all four feet left the porch at the same time. Or, Tiny might run into the yard and bark until she gave away his hiding place.

Tucker held his breath when he saw Tiny emerge from the edge of the wood plank porch and, like a bird in flight, jump to the ground, landing at Mrs. Stuart's feet. Tiny yapped incessantly, each time leaving the sidewalk by several inches and landing in another spot. When he saw Mrs. Stuart was the dog's target, Tucker sighed. *Saved by an eight pound lap dog.* He listened carefully to Gramma and Mrs. Stuart.

"Mrs. Moyer … ah—" Adele Stuart greeted as she walked to the foot of the porch steps.

Tucker scrambled to the end of his hiding pallet, trying to see the conversation.

Mrs. Stuart looked in Tucker's direction and began again. "Thank you for meeting me out here. I'm sorry to call you so early. I know you often rest a while at mid-morning."

"That's all right." Gramma smoothed under some wisps of graying hair that had popped out. "I picked some mint earlier this morning, back there near the hedge row. The water is heating for a nice cup of tea. Joseph is napping."

"Yes…" Adele looked toward the yard again, wrung her hands, and lowered her voice to a whisper. "Mrs. Moyer, now stay calm."

Tucker gasped as his comic book fell from his hand. He grabbed it before it slipped past the edge of the canvas. *Here it comes. Foiled.*

"Calm?" Gramma fixed her hands on her hips. "I am fine. What's happening? I was just calling Tucker because his grandpa needs his help in a while."

"If you'll step out into the yard …" Mrs. Stuart didn't get to finish her difficult message to Gramma.

Suddenly, on the street out front that ran between Elkhart and Goshen, the screech of breaking tires filled the air. Then, another squeal, followed by a thud and crunch as one car plowed into the rear end of another. Tucker could see the back finder of a blue sedan. *Oh no! It's a new car. The fender looks like a 1946.*

Tucker almost fell out of his hiding place when more drivers began screeching to a stop, pointing to the Moyer's side yard. *This is crazy. Everyone is looking at me, and I can't even wave back.* He was too active not to wiggle a little. He stretched up farther to get a better look.

He could see Mrs. Stuart cup her hands to her mouth and jump as another set of tires squealed. Adele's glasses wobbled and slipped from her nose on that hot July day. "Mrs. Moyer, everyone is stopping to gawk because … Tucker is in the walnut tree."

Yikes! Tucker jerked his hat off and rolled up into a knot. *Caught,* he whispered.

"He climbs trees every day," his grandmother dismissed. Tucker could hear the click, click of Gramma's leather shoes as she started down the side steps. "He's a twelve year old boy and …" Rebecca Moyer stopped in mid-stride.

Twenty feet above the side yard, Tucker rocked back and forth in the gentle breeze, deep within the belly of his hammock in the sky. From Gramma's tone, Tucker knew the jig was up.* "Hi, Gramma," he waved. "Whatcha doin'?"

Rebecca Moyer looked up and folded her arms across her body. "What am I doing?" She grabbed the back of her head to protect her stiff neck. High above the ground, Tucker's hammock stretched between the top of the walnut tree and the peak of the two story house, plus an attic. It swayed with the rhythm of his wiggles. "Young man, you get down from there."

Tucker cringed again. "Yes, Gramma."

Turning back to Adele Stewart, she sighed deeply. "That boy has always liked height. When he was five, his cousin went up to get him down off the top of a windmill. Then, Tucker scampered down the other side before Howard could reach him. I think he likes to scare himself … or us. I don't know which." With that she stomped back in the house.

Chapter 2
Unhitched

Tucker knew the plan was awry*. At least, that's what Uncle Jacob would have said. Tucker didn't know what his uncle meant for a long time. Now, it seemed quite appropriate*. His plan was indeed awry. He would have to abandon his day in the sky as a WWII flying ace in his P-51. Gramma had said so.

Freddie Cooper, his good friend and usual cohort in mischief, passed by just as Tucker threw one leg over the side of the hammock, surrendering command of his aircraft. He thought of a parachute jump then decided bailing out without a ripcord wouldn't be realistic.

Freddie, a skinny kid with red hair, scratched his head and hollered, "Hey, Tucker, how'd you get up there?"

A sheepish smile crossed Tucker's face. "I climbed up," he yelled back in a coarse voice, hoping not to draw any more attention. Tucker thought about the moves he'd have to make to get down. The canvas hammock swayed above the ground. A robin fluttered over to the sky–lounge and balanced himself on a stack of Tucker's comic books. Tucker wondered if the bird would leave droppings all over his favorite graphic heroes.

"Why didn't ya call me?" Freddie said more softly, sounding disappointed. "My number is still one long and four shorts*." He and Tucker did a lot of stuff together.

Tucker's friend, Christy also came to see what all the fuss was about. The neighborhood was abuzz with rumors of the flying hammock. She shielded her eyes from the sun as she looked up and called out, "Sure would have liked to have seen the earth from where you are."

Freddie's expression slid down his face and settled in his shoes. "Too late," he complained to Christy. "He's gotta get down."

Tucker knew his stunt could have been the highlight of the summer… a pre-July fourth extravaganza. He cupped his hands to his mouth, loudly apologizing, "Sorry, Freddie … you too, Christy."

"Yes, I know you got up there, but how'd you do it?" Freddie shifted from one bare foot to the other.

"Looks like the bottom of your feet are burning, Freddie." Tucker observed his friend fire-walking on the pavement. "Stand on the grass."

"Was just about to." Freddie hopped onto the cool green of Moyer's lawn.

Christy studied the rigging and sighed. "Fiddle de dee, Freddie. Can't you see how he strung that thing?"

"It was easy," Tucker bragged. "I used Grandpop's heavy rope. Connected one end of the hammock to a long piece of the heavy line, then attached that to a large lag screw* up near the attic. I reached it from the upstairs window. Then I tied the other end to another length of rope and knotted that to the top of the walnut tree. It's thirty feet from the tree to the house-top."

"Crackers, Tucker. You really did it." Christy's eyes were wide.

Tucker's sister, Betsy hadn't seen his contraption until just then when she ran out into the yard. "You're always in trouble, Little Brother." She doubled over with laughter.

Tucker laughed right back. "You get into trouble too, Betsy. You're always dressed in non-Gramma approved outfits."

Betsy was barefoot and had on older brother, Tim's out-grown jeans she had rolled up almost to her knee. Her top was a red T-shirt. "Hey, Fly Boy, after you put away all that stuff, Gramma wants you to come in the house for a little talk."

"Okay," he grumbled. "Big sisters," Tucker mumbled to himself, "not one, but two." He plopped back down on the hammock, took a deep breath, and then took another look.

"Hey Tucker," Christy barked back with her hands on her hips. "I'm a girl, too, ya know."

"You're not a sister-girl. You're a friend-girl." Tucker peered again over the edge. From his vantage point, he saw many folks from the neighborhood, all gathering to see the boy in the sky. Even Pastor Daily, who lived in the parsonage two houses down, came up to see what all the hub-bub was about.

"Tucker," the pastor pointed to where the rope connected to one of the forks high in the tree. "It looks like that knot is coming out." Pastor Daily often called Tucker, the Dunlap Kid, since he was all over the neighborhood. The whole world seemed to belong to Tucker McBride.

"Thanks, Pastor." Tucker lay back for a minute longer in the middle of his sky-high bunk. The blue sky over head was brilliant. Robins higher up in the tree scolded him for making his bed in their house. The seeming concert of buzzing and clicking insects was like music to his ears.

He had planned to relax up there all day, above the disappointment in the house. Still, Gramma had spoken.

Freddie watched as Tucker began to abandon his flight plan. "Can I help you, Tuck?" he yelled.

"Me too," Christy chimed in. "Just tell me what to do."

"Here, Christy," Tucker said as he thought up his mayday plan to ditch his airplane. He took off his belt and wrapped it around his stack of comic books. "I'll drop these down to you. You stand back so you don't get hit, then grab them up before they get dirty."

"Roger that, Captain," Christy said saluting.

Tucker wiggled around in the hammock, unbuckling his belt. Wrapping the leather around his bundle of comics and cinching them in, he aimed them in Christy's direction on the ground.

"Got them," she called back as she snatched them out of the grass. Pulling the belt from around the bundle, she quickly released the ten cent books so they wouldn't get a permanent wrinkle or fold in the paper.

Tucker climbed out of the hammock, then shimmied, hand-over-hand, along the rope to where he had tied it to the walnut tree. He saw where it had slipped, and brushed off any possible danger. Nothing scared Tucker McBride. Getting ready to throw the end of the rope to the ground, he hollered to Freddie, "Don't try to catch it. It might hit you in the head."

"What ya mean, Tuck? You know I can catch any baseball you can throw."

"Yeah, sometimes though you have to ice down your hands after the game." Tucker said with a grin. "Now, untie the end of the rope from the hammock. I'll be right there." With that end of the hammock on the ground, Tucker bounded down out of the tree, one limb at a time.

To unhitch the rope from where it attached to the house, he would have had to go through the house. That was out of the question. He didn't want to face Gramma until he had finished putting everything away like she had told him.

"Okay, now what?" Christy surveyed the other end of the hammock and waited for orders.

"The maple tree," he pointed to the summer kitchen. "I've climbed that tree so many times I can scramble up the trunk blindfolded."

"All right, Tucker." Christy stood at the bottom of the trunk. "We'll spot ya."

Tucker snickered. "Are you going to catch me if I fall?"

Christy squared her shoulders. "No, I'm going to let you splat on the ground and then tell your grandma to call for help."

Tucker's smile was mischievous. "I'd just bounce." He turned and crossed the yard with Christy and Freddie behind him, ready to be part of the continuing adventure.

Approaching the tree with a hop, he threw his left leg up over the first limb. He dangled upside down for a second until he hoisted himself up to a higher crook in the tree. From there, he shinnied out on a low hanging limb and dropped onto the roof of the summer kitchen. Then, he climbed up Uncle Jerry's old ham radio tower to the second floor, and stepped over onto the outside edge of the window sill to his bedroom. Standing on the sill, he reached up to the helpful lag screw above his window, near the attic.

"Well, hello, Tiny." Tucker tapped on the window screen as the dog put her nose on the mesh. Tiny yipped and pranced around Tuck's room, on the floor, on his bed, up and down and around.

"I'll be in there in a minute." *Probably won't get out of my room for a week,* he whispered to the dog. Tucker pulled on the tightened knot until the rope was free. "It's coming down," he called to the two below.

"Freddie can catch it this time," Christy assured him. "I'll grab it the next time you build an oasis in the sky."

"Good thinking," Tucker agreed. Swinging the rope and dangling hammock high and wide, he let it fly out and watched it land on the ground.

Tucker scooted back down the way he came up, grabbed the rope and looped it over his shoulder. "Freddie, you take the other piece."

Christy folded her arms in front of her and snapped. "Why Freddie? You think I can't do it?"

Tucker looked up befuddled. "No … I mean yes …. No, I mean Freddie's arms are longer."

"Well … okay," Christy drew out slowly.

Freddie watched as Tucker wrapped the rope around and under his elbow. He did the same with the other length of rope and followed Tuck to his grandfather's workshop on the edge of the garden.

Inside, the shop smelled of sawdust and finishing oil. The boys hung the coils of rope on the six-by-six inch center beam. Finally, Tucker had no more excuses. Gramma waited inside.

"Gotta go in and face Gramma. See ya later ... I hope." Tucker drug his feet back to the house. He had to admit, he just might be in a bit of trouble. Still, he believed the high-rise hammock was worth the possible consequence of staying in the house for a while. The payoff was not just the excitement of swaying above the earth, but it was also making a plan, working the plan, and accomplishing the task. He would measure the trouble he was in once he heard what Gramma had to say.

Chapter 3
Tea for Tucker

Tucker cautiously eased in through the side door off the little porch, not letting the screen bang behind him. Gramma was sitting on her round piano stool playing the piano. Her long homemade housedress clung to the sides of her legs. The hem length was more in keeping with 1916 than 1946. Tucker stood for a moment and let Gramma's music calm his jitters. What was she going to say? Grandpop's head bobbed up and down to the music, but Tucker suspected he was actually asleep in his big leather Morris chair. Nothing seemed to wake him up once he was napping.

Tiny sat under the old upright piano just beside Gramma's right pedal foot. The little dog's ears twitched to the beat of the hymn she was practicing for Sunday services the next day, *Amazing Grace.*

The rattle and clang of the west bound train reverberated along the tracks a few blocks beyond the house. For some reason, it sounded forlorn to Tucker. Perhaps the train echoed the feelings that hid inside him. *I didn't do anything, I was just having fun.*

Tucker finally spoke up. "Gramma?" His whispered voice was hoarse. "Am I a wretch, like the song says?"

"An unhappy scoundrel?" Gramma swirled around on the piano stool, her eyebrows raised, and her eyes wide. "Tucker McBride, you are one of the happiest boys I know." She spun back again and put her hands on the black keys. Her hands were too small to span the white and black ones, so she poised her fingers over the top of the dark keys so she could reach them. "You're more like this." Beginning a familiar song, she sang, "I've got the joy, joy, joy, joy down in my heart…"

His spirits lifted a little. "That's me, Gramma?"

"That's you, more than anybody I know. Tucker, you daresn't* do such outlandish things as building a swing in the sky, or stretching the facts just to scare us. You know, Grandpa is eighty-five years old. He deserves a peaceful day … at least once in a while."

"Yes, Ma'am," Tucker agreed.

"Now Tucker, after lunch we'll have guests in the house. The pastor and choir from the A.M.E Church in town are coming to practice. They're going to sing tomorrow morning during the service, and I'll play for them. We'll practice here at the house about 2 PM. I'll need you to wash up and change your T-shirt."

"The African Methodists are coming here?" Tucker was excited. He hadn't seen Johnny Washington since Gramma's choir sang at their church during Easter season. "Will Johnny come?"

"Ja*, I suppose. His momma directs the choir." Gramma got up, folded her glasses and put them on the top of the piano. "Now later, when I say, 'Tucker, where'd I put my specs?' You say, 'They're on the piano, Grandma.'" She walked over to the living room and patted the back of one of the chairs that flanked the couch.

Tucker's shoulders wilted a little as he slowly approached his Gramma's small antique settee in front of the large window. He always remembered not to call anything in the Moyer home antique. The Moyers didn't see things that way. Rose marble-topped Victorian tables clustered around chairs and a couch, with Gramma seated in the center of it all. "Gramma?" he asked quietly.

"Tucker," she repeated and waved her hand at the empty chair beside her.

"Are ya mad?" he asked, slouching down in the chair. His blue and white striped cotton T-shirt showed evidence of his morning adventure. A small tear under his arm matched the rip in the lower edge of the shirt. Smudges of this and that dotted the front.

His grandmother looked the boy over from his messy hair to his high-top clodhopper shoes.* "Did you change your clothes before you went exploring?"

Tucker looked down at his shirt and ironed the top of his jeans with the palm of his hands. They looked fine to him. "Yes, Ma'am. Kicking-around clothes are different from school clothes and school clothes are different from Sunday clothes."

"That's good," she said with a quiet smile. "Wait. Is that blood on your hand?"

Tucker checked the side of his left hand. "Looks like a sliver." He tried to squeeze out the tiny piece of wood from the bark on the hammock-holding tree, but nothing came out.

"Go wash your hands, Tucker. Next thing you know you'll get dirt in it." Gramma's voice was low and calm. "Be careful, we mopped the kitchen floor yesterday. Ya daresn't splash all over."

"Okay, Gram."

"Put some Grandma Hooley drawing salve on it while you're out there. Better cover it with a band aid to hold the salve close to the sliver before you come back. The salve will draw that splinter right out."

Tucker lifted the cast iron pump handle on the water pump at the kitchen sink and washed his hands. He applied the salve and band aid he took from the cabinet, and returned to the living room.

Gramma sat back. "I was wondering, Tucker. When did you decide to tie the hammock to the clouds? You know I want you to be safe."

"I was safe, Gramma," he protested as he sat up straighter in the chair to add strength to his argument.

"Ja, ja, Tucker. I want you to think about that," Gramma whispered as she poured two cups of mint tea. She placed her cup on the table and handed the other one to Tucker.

He brought the tea to his lips and inhaled the aroma of summer. Sipping the mint tasting tea, he decided to add a teaspoon of sugar and stirred. "Well, I've thought about it, Gramma." He rested the saucer on his knee. "I'm sure I was safe," he concluded.

Gramma put down her spoon and drank from her fancy china cup. "I was thinking and had questions, too, Tucker," she said, speaking slowly. "Can you tell me what you were doing or what you were thinking and feeling just before you decided to string the hammock twenty feet above the ground?"

"Hum," he tried to think of words he thought Gramma would accept. "Are you sure I was twenty feet off the ground?"

"Ja, Tucker, twenty feet."

"Well … what was I thinking?" He closed his eyes and rehearsed the events since breakfast. "Oh, I remember. Carolyn showed me a story in the newspaper that said the Concord School's baseball field is going to have Fourth of July fireworks on Thursday, to celebrate all the guys who came home from the war."

"I heard about that," Gramma said as she pulled the paper from under the pillow beside her. "Your sister showed it to me. Let's have a look."

"Right there," Tucker pointed to a front page article under the center fold.

"Aunt Franny and I talked about the fireworks. Your cousin Howard will be here and ready to celebrate being home. That's why we're having the picnic on the fourth."

Tucker thought about his cousin's service in the Navy during the war. While Howard was older than Tucker, all of the family was close. Tucker thought again. "That makes sense." Then he stopped, hoping the steam building up inside him would cool down. "But Joe was in the war too, and the Army didn't let him come home."

"Joe?" Gramma asked, puzzled. "Joe is a dog."

"Our dog," Tucker protested pounding his fist on the arm of the chair. "Uncle Jacob *loaned* Joe to the Army for the K-9 Corps. They were supposed to give him back after the war. Joe got hurt, and all they gave Uncle Jacob were his medals … the Silver Star for bravery and the Purple Heart for his wounds. It's not fair."

"So, to keep your temper down, you decided to organize a large project … a hammock up high in the sky to hide in." She picked up the tea pot and poised it over the cup. "More tea?" she asked him.

"Tea? No." He sat back in his chair. *Hide?* He lowered his eyes and wiggled around in his chair. "Was I hiding?"

Gramma nodded. "I was wondering if your temper might be that Irish blood in you … the McBrides are Irish."

Tucker's mouth dropped open. "Is it a bad thing to be Irish?"

"Heavens no," she gasped. "The Irish and Pennsylvania Dutch can both be stubborn, but the Irish don't argue about it like the Pennsylvania Dutch. They just quietly think they're right. The Irish are very warm and friendly people. They'll talk to everyone. Your momma's Pennsylvania Dutch side is organized and hard working." Her eyes brightened, "Maybe you're stubborn side was fighting with your worker side. When you ran into the big disappointment today, thinking about Joe, rather than getting mad, you controlled yourself by getting to work on your hammock project."

Tiny wiggled at Tucker's feet before she jumped up on his lap and waited for a tummy rub. Tucker began to relax as he petted her on her underbelly. He opened his blue eyes wide. "Is that what happened?"

"I think so. Since you have more energy than two people, but have trouble paying attention, you just wrap yourself up in a creative project you enjoy and work hard to meet your goal." She finished her tea and placed the cup on its saucer. "The thing is, Tucker, I would think you might like to learn to stay out of trouble."

"Oh, yes, Ma'am," Tucker agreed. Gramma had a way of finding the problem and solution all at the same time.

"I think if you take a minute to talk with me or your grandpa before you start one of your undertakings, we can help you. Together, we can guide you into making a safe plan. Work can distract you from anger or disappointment."

"Thanks, Gramma. I'll try that." He jumped up and started for the stairs.

"Tucker… don't run in the house. Or … are you hiding from something again?"

"Well, maybe one thing." He put both hands on the oak newel post at the base of the stair railing and threw his feet out to the side perpendicular to the floor, like a circus act under the big top.

"I'll overlook the gymnastics for now. I want to know what you're thinking."

Tucker stuffed his hands in his pockets. "Joe was the best German Shepherd anyone ever had. To me he was even more than that. He was part of our family. Since he's been gone, our house seems empty. Joe didn't die in the war. He should have come home."

"Then, that's your new job, Tucker. To make peace with the fact that Joe didn't come home. You have family all around you. Cousins are all over, up and down the street, in your school, and in your church."

Tucker hung his head. "I know, but it feels different." What he didn't want to tell her was his cousins and friends had moms and dads in their family. He didn't. His mom died and his dad couldn't take care of him and his three siblings.

"Now, if you want a creative project to help you concentrate, your Uncle Jacob's birthday is coming up, also on the fourth of July. That's just five days away. We have no extra money. We still have to get food for the family picnic on the fourth. But … talk to your grandpa when he wakes up from his nap. He can help you think of something to make for Uncle Jacob … without cutting off your fingers."

"Okay, Gramma," Tucker agreed. Again his thoughts raced around in his head like a hamster on an exercise wheel.

"Remember Tucker, stubbornness can change into steadfastness, when you take the anger out of it." Gramma gathered up the tea dishes and started for the kitchen.

Tucker wrinkled up his nose. "Steadfastness?"

Gramma smiled. "Steadfastness means you're stubborn enough to get a job done, but you don't have to get mad about it. With your creativity, and the light of joy around you, you can do it."

He liked Gramma's idea. Tucker also knew the problem wouldn't be in thinking up the project or getting it started. The problem would be in finishing the job. Would he learn to be steadfast before the fourth of July?

Chapter 4
Johnny and Tucker

That afternoon would be all that Tucker could hope for, full of song, sweet lemonade, and Grandma Dunn's nutmeg sugar cookies. To Tucker's way of thinking, nothing could be better. He tried to slip one of the cookies from the large platter Gramma had artfully arranged them on, but decided Gramma would notice. They looked yummy and, equally important, they were really big. If he moved one of the cookies, the empty spot would scream, "cookie thief!" After he counted them carefully and determined there were at least two a piece, he decided it was safe to wait. In the kitchen, his search of the cabinets also found Gramma's private stash. He forgot how many cookies Grandma Dunn's recipe makes. He figured Gramma had made enough, whatever that was. The rest of the sugary goodness, covered with one of Gramma's fancy embroidered tea towels, was stored in a large crock on the corner of the blue linoleum-covered kitchen counter.

"An adequate amount," Tucker nodded with a smile and a whisper. He also knew Gramma well enough to know if the number of cookies on the platter disappeared fast, she would send him to the crock to add more to the large plate.

Since his grandmother expected company that afternoon, she changed her baking day from Saturday to Friday. Seven fresh fruit pies and seven loaves of yeasty smelling homemade bread waited in the pie safe in the corner of the dining room, one for each day of the week. Whatever cookies remained after the company left, Gramma would put back in the crock, free for family members to partake. If there were still some the next day she'd have

Grandpop carry the crock to the basement where it was dry and cool. However, she made the mistake of storing a large tin of lard there too. When Tucker was really hungry, he'd sneak a tablespoon down there to spoon out some lard. Gramma wondered why the lard was going down faster than she used it. It never occurred to her that anyone would eat lard straight from the can.

"Tucker?" Christy called from the door off the summer kitchen. "I hear you raiding your grandmother's cookies."

Turning back, Tucker called out, "I'm right here. And, I wasn't raiding. I was inspecting."

"Whatever you think you were doing is fine with me," she agreed. "Can you come out?"

Tucker hurried down the three steps into the attached room where Gramma did her laundry and the whole family took turns bathing in the laundry rinse tub. When they first built the house, Grandpop and his brothers tore down the dwelling that had originally sat on the lot, but kept the summer kitchen and built the new home onto it. Sometimes, Gramma cooked there in the summer in order to keep her wood-burning Wedgewood stove in her fancy turn-of-the-century kitchen from heating up the house. Now, she only did the laundry and the messy job of late summer canning in that room. The ball canning jars, full of peaches and cherries, were then stored on shelves in the coolest corner of the basement.

Tucker saw his friend through the screen door and grinned. "Hi Christy." He opened the door inviting her in. "Come out? Well, Christy, here's the thing."

Christy's smile started to fade. "The thing? Sorry if this isn't a good time."

"No, no," Tucker protested. "Gramma is having the choir from a church in town over to practice for their songs tomorrow."

"Ah," she inhaled slowly. "The game's afoot."

Tucker curled his mouth up at the corner. "What game?"

"It's an expression I heard on *The Lux Radio Theater*." Christy brushed some blond hair from her forehead. "It means the situation is already happening. So, whatever 'the thing' is, you're already committed to it."

Tucker nodded slowly. "The game that is afoot, the 'thing,' is five dozen of the best tasting huge pastries this side of heaven. I am the butler for all of Grandma Dunn's sugar cookies."

"Oh, now I get it," Christy laughed. "Where food is involved, you are close at hand."

"Of course," Tucker bragged with a smile as he held up his biceps like a two fisted weight lifter. "I'm strong but need more meat on my body to show it off."

"Meat, yes," Christy giggled. "A pound of sugar per arm? No. It'll get you a full, round, wobbly arm, not a muscular one."

"I'll endure that humiliation in the future." He looked in the crock again and spotted a very small cookie along the side. "In the meantime, I'll relieve Gramma of her own humiliation, serving a cookie much smaller than the rest." He reached in and pulled out the slightly smaller round scrumptious joy.

"Oh, no you don't," Christy warned as Tucker brought the cookie to his mouth. "If you want me to keep your transgression* a secret...I'll have half of it." She grabbed the cookie, broke it in half and sized the two parts. She gave Tucker the larger portion. "You supplied the cookie, and I'll supply the generous side." She took a bite of the cookie and swooned. "This is wonderful. Who is Grandma Dunn? I never heard you talk about her." She polished off the last bite and brushed the crumbs from her hands.

Tucker laughed. "I never met her. She was Gramma's great-grandmother. That's why Gramma calls them *three generation nutmeg sugar cookies*."

"Oh, good honk," Christy gasped. "I don't think Mom has any recipes that are that old."

"Tucker," Gramma called from the living room.

"Coming Gramma," he nodded at Christy, swallowed every bite, brushed all crumb evidence from his shirt, and went into the living room with Christy close behind. "Gramma, can Christy stay and listen to the choir practice?"

"Ja, of course," Gramma answered while catching a glimpse out the window. "Look across the street. They're here."

Outside, several cars pulled into the church parking lot. The sun had come out and sprayed the yard with bits of sparkling beams. As people piled out of their Ford and Dodge sedans into the sunny afternoon, they laughed and nudged each. The choir walked across the narrow Moyer Avenue to greet Gramma who waited at the door. Grandpop stood up and joined her as the visitors reached the side steps. Any visitor was an honored guest.

Goldie Washington, the choir director, dressed in a breezy red sun dress and large brimmed straw hat with a matching satin ribbon, led the small group. "Rebecca Moyer, my goodness gracious, you look good," Goldie exclaimed, opening her arms for a hug.

"Goldie," Rebecca returned her hug warmly, "it is so good to see you again." She stood back making way for all the choir members to enter the house. Gramma wrapped her arm around Goldie's waist. "I was so sorry to hear about your loss."

"I know, thanks friend. It's been a year but it's still hard."

Rebeca patted Goldie's back. "Your husband was such a good man, a hard worker, involved in the community and the church."

"Tucker," Gramma said as she turned, "would you and Christy get the cookies and lemonade?"

"Sure, Gramma." Tucker smiled a cookie-fiend grin. "See, I told ya," he whispered to Christy. "There was a reason why you came over this afternoon."

Christy beamed. "I actually smelled the cookie all the way at my house."

Together, they brought in the authentic, Tucker-approved sugary cookies, the tall glass pitcher of sweet-tart lemonade, small juice glasses, little dessert plates, and white cloth napkins. His grandmother had used her fine needle art to embroider a tiny rose in the corner of each cloth. They placed all the fixings on the table and stepped back.

"This is fun." Christy giggled. "My mom doesn't serve refreshments, no matter who comes. Come to think of it, Mom doesn't entertain very much."

Tucker wondered about that. Didn't everyone have a parade of visitors marching through their house every week? He had never thought that his family did special things that other families didn't do.

A man with graying temples came in behind Goldie. Joseph reached out his large hand fitting a man of six foot two inches. "Welcome, Pastor Gleason," Grandpop greeted him with a handshake and a broad smile.

"Thank you for having us, Joseph." Pastor Gleason returned both the smile and the warm grip of his hand.

As each member of the A.M.E. Church passed by the dining room table, they put a cookie or two on their plate and poured a half glass of lemonade. Everyone murmured their own oohs and aahs, followed by semi-silence as each guest found a chair and nibbled on their cookies.

Goldie's son, Johnny Washington, came in last. A little shorter than Tucker, he was a muscular, jovial kid. "Hold up there," Johnny called out when he came in the door. "Don't take those cookies out of here until I get some."

Tucker saw his grandmother's nod. "Hi, Johnny," Tucker said as he kept going with the plate. "Come on out here."

"It's okay, Johnny. Have fun." One of the male choir members gave the boy a wink.

Tucker thought the man probably sang bass, given the deep mellow* tone in the big man's speaking voice. He smiled as he thought about Grandpop and how he could vibrate the church pew on some of the deepest notes of the hymns.

The three went out to the kitchen to load up the plate again. Tucker stopped, "Oh sorry. This is Christy Tree, and Christy, this is Johnny Washington."

"Christy Tree?" Johnny eyes sparkled with mischievous. "Is that short for Christmas Tree?"

"Maybe…" she glared at him with her hands on her hips. "I answer *only* to Christy."

"And, she means it." Tucker said seriously and smiled a crooked smile.

His grandmother came out into the kitchen just as Tucker put another dozen cookies on the platter. "Thank you, Tuck. Now, you three gather up a few of those sweet delights for yourself and go have some fun."

"Thanks Gramma." Tucker reached into the crock, handed two to Christy, two to Johnny, and drew out two for his own enjoyment, although four or five would have been a better number. "Hey, I know what we can do." He waved his arm in a "follow me" gesture.

He led the way through the living room and started up the stairs just as the choir began to warm up. "Christy, you'll be able to hear them practice from up here."

The other two followed as Tucker walked down the upstairs hall, into his bedroom. "Through here." He opened his closet door and shoved some shirts back revealing some steps tucked in behind shorter hanging clothes to the right.

The steps led to the attic where the family had stored a lifetime of nitpickies and fudduddles.

"Oh wow!" Christy gasped as they stepped onto the rougher floor boards of the full attic. "Look at all this stuff."

Of all the boxes and trunks in the attic, three groups were Tucker's favorites: the boxes of family pictures dating back several generations and large photographs of train accidents involving bridges. Since Grandpop had been the foreman of the bridge building crew for the New York Central railroad, he had many examples of him and his men repairing the wooden structures. The other group of nifty items that Tucker could read over and over was Uncle Jacob's *National Geographic Magazines.* He knew his uncle had placed every back issue all together along the sloping eaves, in the order of their publication. Tucker reached up and pulled the chain Grandpop had attached to the light that hung from the center of the beamed ceiling. The attic came alive with light, not so much to make it glare, just enough to add intrigue.

"Oh wow, *National Geographic,*" Johnny beamed. "Help me find the September issue from last year."

"Sure," Tucker agreed.

Christy joined in the search for the specific issue. "Have you seen that magazine before? What's so special about it?"

"Yeah, I've seen it. The city library has every issue. I remember there's an article in the September one about some generals, Patton, Eisenhower and some others, who found some Nazis' gold in a salt mine at Merkers, Germany." He stopped as his eyes glazed over. "My dad was killed near Merkers as the troops marched in to secure the city. I still read everything I can about that area, sometimes over and over. I feel like I'm a little closer to Dad when I read articles and see pictures of where he'd been. I want to see it all again."

"Johnny … I didn't know," Tucker whispered. "I hadn't heard anybody talk about it." He was embarrassed; he didn't know that Mr. Washington had died in the war. Grandpop listened to the news every night, so Tucker was aware of the long war but he knew it wasn't that way in some homes. Parents of some of his friends shielded them from news of the battles.

Johnny smiled a little. "My mother couldn't listen to the news. It only made her worry more and wish Dad were home.

Christy stuck her hands in her pockets. "I am so sorry, Johnny."

"That's okay. The newsreels at the movie theater had very little footage about black G.I.'s serving in the war. Many of the guys were heroes but no one knows it." Johnny's expression fell into despair. "My dad was part of the final push into Germany as that crazy man's grip on Europe was winding down. Dad's unit was in the Merkers area when a sniper's bullet hit him."

Tucker angrily bit off a big bite of cookie, like a lion ripping into a hunk of meat. "That guy over there was a dummkopf*," Tucker's eyebrows furrowed in disgust.

"Dummkopf?" Christy and Johnny asked in unison.

Tucker knew he had spoken before he thought. "Sorry. It means stupid idiot." He looked down quickly. "Don't tell Gramma I said that word."

"Of course not," Johnny pledged, his hand on his heart.

Christy smiled in support. "Word's spoken in the attic can be caustic. Don't repeat."

Johnny smiled slightly, "Did you just make that up?"

"She's some kind of poet," Tucker shrugged. He chomped off a bite of the second cookie as he handed the magazine to Johnny.

Johnny leafed through the National Geographic as if he had the page number memorized. Tucker watched as tears gathered in his friend's eyes.

Tucker realized he was complaining that he didn't have a family like other kids. Johnny had a family, but the ravages of war destroyed it. Then Johnny's church stepped in to help his mother and became his larger family. Tucker's family was always there in the white house on the corner. Everyone else in the neighborhood was a relative by blood or by love. He wondered…*What is a family anyway?*

Chapter 5
A Trip to Goshen

After Johnny and the other friends from the visiting choir walked back across the street and piled into their cars, Tucker and Christy sat on the top step of the side porch and waved. The cars hummed; the smell of gas hung in the air, and they pulled out of the parking lot as the spatter of gravel scattered everywhere.

"That was fun." Tucker watched as the three-car procession pulled onto the highway.

Christy's eyes glowed with the satisfaction of an afternoon well spent. "You have the most interesting family. Very few people ever come to our house."

"Really?" Tucker was amazed. "At our house, there's always somebody, family or friends. Before I was born, Gramma's cousin and her husband lived here with them. Gramma used to feed hobos who rode the boxcars and hopped off the train up there on the tracks."

Tucker pointed to the railroad crossing where, many years ago, his grandfather would jump off the train at the end of his workweek. "The engine would slow down, and Grandpop would step off while the cars continued to rattle along the tracks. The following Monday, he would slip back on. He never learned to drive a car," Tucker shrugged. "The train, or now the interurban*, takes him where he wants to go."

Christy's mouth hung open in surprise. "Your grandmother fed people she didn't even know?"

"Sure." Tucker was amazed that Christy was surprised. "Gramma told me stories of life in the Depression years. Sometimes, she'd come downstairs early in the morning and find a guy dressed in old clothes and tattered shoes, sitting here on this very step. She'd fix him a fried egg sandwich using her thick, homemade bread." Tucker smiled as he thought about the yeasty smell of the bread he ate every day.

Christy shook her head in amazement. "Wow, my mom would never do that. She would be afraid to talk to a scruffy looking guy, let alone fix him breakfast." Her eyes brightened as she thought of another possibility. "Maybe your grandfather knew him or any of the others who stopped by, from when they were riding the rails. Maybe he told a few down-on-their-luck travelers, if they were in the area, they could get a little food here at your house."

"Never thought of that." Tucker quickly stood up so Uncle Jacob could pass. He saw his uncle's keys in his hand. "Where ya going?"

"The Boy Scouts dropped a few more bundles of newspapers for the paper drive on the front porch while the choir practiced." He kept on walking to his car. "The papers are bound up and stacked but they missed the collection the stake truck* already hauled away. I'm going to take the final donation over to Goshen. You two want to help me load them in the trunk?"

Uncle Jacob's car was a 1939 Studebaker coupe. Designed for business men, coupes had huge trunks. The salesmen could load many samples and products for delivery in the over-sized space. "You two can go to Goshen with me if you help put the papers in the car."

"Wow," Tucker started toward the car before Christy got off the step. "Christy can go, too?"

"With her parents' permission," Uncle Jacob said without missing a step.

Gramma stood at the door watching the choir leave and enjoying the day. Overhearing the newspaper drive conversation, she joined in. "Tucker, you can go. I'll call your mother, Christy, and see if it's all right if you go along."

Christy turned around and gasped, "Swell, Mrs. Moyer. Our telephone number is two longs, two shorts and a long."

"Ja, gut*," Gramma said. "And, Tucker, going to Goshen will work out gut for your Uncle James, too. Remember, you promised him you'd help with his demonstration of front line medic care at the 4H fair in a few weeks. He called to say he's going to do a practice run at the Independence Week mini fair in Goshen today, if you can be there. I'll call him and tell him you're on your way over there if you think you can help him out. It'll be about 5 PM. You would be home in time for supper."

"Sure," Tucker thought about what he and Uncle James had rehearsed. "It'll be fun." He smiled. Inside, he did a hand stand. He liked to rattle people and this was another chance at mischief.

"I'd like to see your demonstration," Christy agreed as she reached over and shook Tucker's arm.

"Ja gut. The police know Uncle James from his Boy Scout work. I'll ring the call station over there." Gramma thumped the screen door in conclusion and went back to the crank phone*.

Jacob opened the driver's door and turned back. "I'll go around the block and pull up at the front porch. You two meet me there."

"Will do." Tuck started running around to the front side of the house as he made a giant circular *follow me* gesture with his hand. Christy ran after him.

The sky was so blue and clear Tucker couldn't take his eyes off the heavens. Suddenly, a rumble above them caused him to jerk to attention. "That's it!"

"*It* what?" Christy asked as she looked up, stretched, and shielded her eyes with her hand.

Tucker grinned and spun around in excitement. "Grandpop said the paper reported a B-36 was going to fly over this area, on the way to Dayton, Ohio for inspection. It's the new bomber they're preparing for active duty."

"Thought those things were kept secret." Christy kept her eyes fixed on the massive airplane.

"It's only about five-hundred feet off the ground and roaring so loud it makes my bones rattle. I don't think it's much of a secret." Tucker waved at the plane as it approached their back yard. "Look Uncle Jacob. See it?" he shouted.

"Couldn't miss it," Uncle Jacob said laughing.

The pilot tipped the wings of the huge aircraft, waving back. Tucker jumped up and down with excitement. "Someday…" he beamed. "Someday I'll fly."

Tucker stumbled a little as he turned and refocused. At the front steps, he skidded to a stop and stared. On the right side of the large front porch the Scouts placed several three foot stacks of newspapers bound in the same twine they came delivered in.

Tucker and Christy would have to help Uncle Jacob move the papers as quickly as possible. About four PM each day, a truck from the Elkhart Truth Newspaper would drop off all the papers for delivery in the Dunlap area on the Moyer's front porch. Newsboys and girls with paper routes would gather on the porch floor to sort and roll their share of papers.

"Why does the newspaper truck drop off the papers here?" Christy asked as she sized up the stacks of papers.

Tucker pointed to the little grocery store across the street. "They used to deliver the bundles to the steps over there. If it rained, the news carriers got wet while they folded their share for their paper route. Grandpop made a deal with them. He gave his permission for the truck to drop off the newspapers here on our porch where the kids would be out of any bad weather. In exchange, they gave Grandpop the string the bundles came wrapped in. He made a jig* to weave the string into rope."

"Wow," Christy was amazed. "Your grandfather can do anything."

Jacob hurried up the steps and studied the situation. "We don't want the old newspapers to get mixed up with today's issue." He spread his arms in a general measure of the size of the stacks. "Since there's no back seat in the car, the trunk is big. I think about three fourths of these papers will fit in there. I hope we can put the rest of them on the wide ledge behind the front seat."

Jacob opened the trunk that waited like Jonah's open-mouth whale. Tucker picked up three bundles at a time. Christy carried one. Jacob picked up the rest.

"I suppose you think I'm a weakling," Christy sputtered.

Tucker stopped and looked over the top of the stacks in his arms. "Nope. I'm glad you can help. Three pairs of hands make the job go faster."

In a matter of minutes, they pushed in the last bundle that could possibly fit in the trunk. "Okay." Jacob dusted his hands together and smiled. "Just those few to go and they should fit on the ledge."

Together they finished packing the car when Tucker's grandmother came out onto the front porch. "I got ahold of your mother, Christy. She said you can go along. She'll keep your dinner in the oven on warm if you're late."

"Swell, Mrs. Moyer. That's super. Thanks."

All three climbed into the coupe and headed south on Route 33 to Goshen. They drove past house after house of people Tucker knew as he named each one. Then they passed the airport where several small airplanes waited on the dirt runway for lift off and a Saturday afternoon in the air.

Once in Goshen, Jacob pulled into Elkhart County's collection and distribution center where a large rollup door stood open. Tucker could see that the warehouse was full of stacks and stacks of papers of all kinds and sizes.

"What is all of this paper stuff?" Christy gulped.

Tucker peered into the space. "We collected papers during the war for a ton of things the military needed. Since the war is over, I'm not sure what they're using the stuff for."

Jacob sat facing the loading dock until he got a man's attention inside. "This is the rest of the paper drive from the Boy Scout Troop at Concord School. I have the first paperwork you supplied when the troop leader dropped off the major load. The troop number is on the paper."

"Good, good," the warehouse foreman announced and flopped his folder closed. He held out his hand. "I'm Granger. If you can wait, I'll have the boys weigh it all and make out a check payable to the troop."

Jacob looked at Tucker and Christy. "How long will that take?"

The foreman looked again at the papers with all the bundles put together, the previous load, and the current one. "Hmm … thirty to forty-five minutes. We close at five."

Jacob checked his watch. "It's four fifteen. We'll come back before you close at five … in about thirty to forty minutes."

"Good, good," Granger repeated.

The three piled into the desert colored Studebaker and gathered a new plan. "Let's go into town." Jacob backed out of the parking lot, turned left, then down about a half mile and turned right onto N. Main Street, into Goshen's business district.

Jacob pointed to the Olympia Candy Kitchen on the left side of the road. "I'll give you a couple of dollars for candy. Your grandpa really likes hard tack. Get him a fourth pound. A Coca-Cola will be five cents each, so ten cents would work for both of you. That would leave some money for any candy you two might want."

"Okay," Tucker grinned at Christy. Any candy sounded good to him. Like Grandpop, he liked fruit flavored ribbons and other hard candy, especially the multi-colored pieces you find in small boxes of Christmas hard tack. He stopped thinking about sweets and asked Jacob, "Where will you be?"

"I'm going down to Garland's Department Store to get a new shirt for church. Tiny tore mine when I was playing with her last Sunday." Jacob drove past the block that had the candy store and Garland's in the same stretch of buildings. "I'll go down and turn around so I can park on the same side of the street."

A quick turn around the block and he slowed the Studebaker. "I'll park closer to the department store since you'll go up there when you're done."

Tucker was silent as they walked back to the sweet shop. His mind however, was racing. *Garland's? What if I see Dad? Do I introduce him to Christy or ignore him? Christy might think I'm ashamed of her if I don't say something.*

Finally, Christy broke the silence. "Mr. Moyer never said why the warehouse was going to pay the Boy Scouts for old newspapers."

"When they collected papers for the war drive, there was no payment. Everybody was trying to help the boys in the war any way they could. This is different. They'll pay the Boy Scouts for this load."

Once they got to the Olympia Candy Kitchen, Tucker pulled the door open for Christy. "Many guys came home from the war and couldn't find a place to live. Contractors had to get busy and build tons of new houses. The salvage company will sell the old papers to a company that will chop them up, treat the particles with fire retardant, and turn it into home insulation."

Christy stepped into the store and smiled. "So, the Boy Scouts gets a percentage of what the salvage company gets? Snazzy!" Her eyes popped as she looked around the store. "This store is snazzy, too."

Chocolates of many kinds, displayed in a series of glass bens, lined the right side of the store. They made Tucker's mouth water. Sparkling jars of penny candy sat on top of the row of light and dark chocolates. Tucker paced slowly back and forth in front of the display, trying to decide what he wanted.

Christy's smile spilled over. "I know what I want … Chocolate covered peanuts."

"We're ready to order," Tucker spoke to the clerk. "We'll have a fourth pound of hard tack, a fourth pound of chocolate covered peanuts, a fourth pound of licorice whips, and two cokes in the bottle, with straws."

The clerk, dressed in a cocoa brown dress and sensible shoes, prepared three white paper sacks of the candy and set out two six and a half ounce bottles of Coca-Cola. Tucker paid the lady and popped the top of his bottle on the opener near the door. Christy did the same.

Outside, they walked slowly along the wide sidewalk up toward Garland's. It was a perfect day in every way…except one. Tucker wasn't very interested in seeing his father. His discomfort was itchy. So he focused on other things. He watched the cars that puttered, sputtered and hummed by. The courthouse, up in the next block and across the street, was decked out with American flag bunting on every lamp posts. Dotted around the court yard, tents provided shelter for interesting scenarios for public display and discussion. Some vendors had started early selling hotdogs and popcorn. He could smell the warm butter a half block away.

Tucker smiled at the blackbirds that flew overhead and flocked in the courthouse trees. The *conk-la-ree** of the red-winged birds that flitted from tree to tree took Tucker's mind off what might be waiting for him at Garland's.

Tucker took as long as possible to walk down the sidewalk, without actually sitting cross legged on the hot concrete. He was dragging his feet so much, Christy asked, "Something wrong?"

Tucker wondered how much he was willing to talk about. "My dad works at Garland's."

Christy listened to the silence that followed and then asked, "You don't want to talk to him?"

"Not really."

"Tucker…I've wondered…why wasn't your dad in the war? My dad was in a car crash and broke his shoulder. They couldn't take him."

Tucker didn't like to talk about his father so his answer was slow in forming. "When Dad went in for his physical, the doctor said his heart was really enlarged and it wasn't located where it belonged. If Dad got hurt in battle and needed treatment, the medics could have a problem finding it."

Regardless of how confused Tucker felt about his father, when they got to the department store, he started to open the door and then stopped. He decided he would go in, but was in no hurry. He looked in the large front display window but didn't see his dad through the glass.

People walked by and wedged themselves past Tucker who nearly blocked the entrance. "In or out," one man said in a joking tone.

Sean McBride was a gifted man with a special sense of design. He was the one who usually decorated the front window at Garland's. After Tucker paused long enough to search inside the store as far as he could see, he exhaled loudly. The windows were all dressed up for Independence Day in flags, festivities, and fashions.

Christy looked longingly through the glass in the doors. "Can we go in?"

Tucker was determined to overcome his bad feelings about his dad and tried his best to sort out something good in all of it. "Sure, we'll go in. Do you want to look at something or look at everything?"

She clapped her hands together. "Mom said I could buy some shoes with a little heel this fall. I just want to look at them."

"Heels? Christy, all shoes have heels." He held up his clodhopper to show her the clunky leather.

Laughing, she popped him on his arm. "Not those kind, silly … a dressy heel."

Tucker couldn't say anything for a few seconds. Finally, he only repeated himself. "Heels?" He shook his head. "How can you run bases in heels?"

"That's ridiculous," she looked at him in near shock, and laughed. "I wouldn't wear them to play baseball."

Thunder struck by the unbelievable thought of Christy in high heeled shoes, Tucker nearly ran into a man carrying two men's suits on hangers. "Sorry," Tucker apologized in passing, not really noticing the man.

"Tucker?" His dad's smile was huge. "How did you get to Goshen?"

Fumbling and bumbling with his coke and bags of candy, Tucker nearly spilled the soda. "Dad?"

"That's me." Sean reached out and put his hand on Tucker's arm.

"Uncle Jacob brought the last stacks of newspapers from the Boy Scout paper drive into Goshen. The last few bundles didn't arrive in time to make the large load. He said we could come along." He turned to Christy. "Oh, this is Christy Tree."

"John and Mary Tree's daughter?" Sean asked with a big smile on his face.

Christy blinked, surprised. "Yes. Do you know them?"

Sean placed the suits carefully on the counter. "Of course I do. John and I went to school together. He and your mom come in here to shop."

Christy covered her mouth with her hand. "You're the Sean Dad talks about?"

Tucker's mouth flew open. How could that be? How could his dad know people that he and his grandparents know? The Trees go to his church.

"I suppose I am that Sean." He motioned for his customer to come over to the cash register. To the new suit man and his wife, he said, "Hope I'm not slowing you down."

"No, no." Even though the wife was dressed fancier than most women in his family, she still had time for Tucker. "I'm Mrs. Lauderbach. Sean is your father?"

"Yes," was all Tuck could mumble out.

Mrs. Lauderbach smiled. "He's a wonderful man. He often brings our son into town for work when Gabe's car isn't working. Gabe is working here in the stockroom for the summer. He'll be going to college in the fall."

Tucker wasn't able to say anything. He just stood there for a minute until Uncle Jacob came up. "Are you two ready, Tucker?" To the clerk, Jacob added, "Hello Sean."

"I haven't seen the shoes yet," Christy squinted and bounced a little on her toes.

Jacob checked his watch. "I still have to pay Sean for this shirt. So, you can take about ten minutes. Okay?"

"Yes," she squealed. "The shoe department is right over there," she pointed to the back of the store past the perfume department and expensive handbags.

Tucker pulled on the sleeve of her shirt. "I'll go with you."

As the two started toward the back of the store, Jacob told them, "I'll meet you at the front door. In the meantime, I'll visit with Camilla and George Lauderbach."

"Camilla and George?" Tucker whispered to Christy. "Who are Camilla and George? They know my dad and my uncle too. I've never heard of them."

"They know your dad and they like him." Christy stated decidedly.

"Why?" Tucker blustered.

"They say he's a nice guy, Tucker." Christy snapped a little to remind him. "Remember, people see neighbors in different ways."

"But … why is he nice to them?"

"And … not to you?" she asked carefully. "Maybe they don't expect him to be any more than he is, a friend."

At the center back of the store, the shoe department sparkled with styles no one in Tucker's family wore. He had to admit, they sure smelled good. Then, he spotted one pair he thought Carolyn would wear. Looking again, maybe she already had a pair just like them. Tucker picked up some patent leather low heeled pumps and ran his fingers over the high polished leather. "I could agree with these."

Christy turned up her nose. "Because, they're not very high? You expect me to be able to run a little in those?"

"Maybe," he sputtered. "Maybe it's because I like the smell of the sweet leather."

"As we get older, Tucker, will you expect me to always be a tomboy … because that's what you want me to be? Or, in a few years, can I still be your friend? People grow. So has your dad."

"Sure," was all Tucker could say. But inside he wondered … *Do I expect people to be what I want them to be? Or, can I let people become who they want to be and not what I want them to be?*

Chapter 6
Tucker's Version of Wound Care

Across the street, on the wide green of the Courthouse lawn, three tents clustered on the left at the corner where traffic could see the festivities from both directions. The octagonal limestone police telephone center, on the northwest corner of Lincoln Avenue and Main Street, stood four feet above street level, like a bullet-proof sentinel* station over downtown Goshen. Tucker's imagination carried him to the top of castle turrets or to an old-west fort's protective parapet every time he saw the eight-sided structure.

He had to direct his attention away from the intersection and back to the tents. One canvas shelter was a little larger than the other two. Women in bright colored cotton sundresses and men in summer white trousers, milled around on the grass. It was the only day out of the whole year when the city permitted loitering on the courthouse lawn. On a large banner stretched between two flag poles were the words that announced the theme of the display, **SAVING THE SOLDIER.** The largest tent was marked, **STATION HOSPITAL**, the other two, **FIELD HOSPITAL** and **GENERAL HOSPITAL.** James Moyer stood out in front of the Station Hospital tent waving at Tucker.

"Hi Uncle James," Tucker waved back.

Uncle Jacob started walking toward the car with the Garland's sack under his arm. "You two go on over to help James. I'll go back to the warehouse and get the Boy Scouts' payment for the papers. They'll close soon. I'll be back in about twenty minutes."

"Okay," Tucker and Christy said at the same time. Each looked at the other, then raced up to the light at the corner and darted across the street.

It was a dead heat when the light at the crosswalk turned red. Tucker decided no one would be able to tease him for not beating a girl in a little foot race. He'd simply say he'd grown weak from the heavy aroma of elephant ears and caramel corn.

"What is all this?" Christy looked into the open flap at each tent.

"Great. You're here just in time. The police gave me your grandma's message." James nodded toward the display. "The Red Cross wanted to inform the public about how the injured boys were medically treated during the war," he said with an inviting sweep of his arms. "You can learn something different at each tent through annotated pictures and a Q&A opportunity."

Christy looked around bewildered. "What?"

Tucker laughed. "Annotated means pictures with notes and Q&A is questions and answers."

Christy stopped and stomped her foot. "How did you know that, Tucker McBride?"

He grinned back. "National Geographic."

Uncle James was so happy to see Tucker, he slapped him on the back hard enough the boy lurched forward. "Glad you could come."

Quickly straightening up, Tucker laughed, turned and clapped his uncle on the arm with a hearty thump. "This should be fun." If it wasn't, Tucker would find a way to make it so.

There was a smaller sign on the door flap to the tent. **DEMONSTRATION 4:45.** "Hurry up," James motioned with a wave of his hand.

Inside, the olive-drab canvas squad tent was sixteen feet wide, thirty-two feet seven inched long and twelve feet high. Tucker thought it smelled like his Scout Master's garage. Since Uncle James was one of those leaders, Tucker said no more. An Army cot, elevated by a roughly made platform Uncle James had constructed for demonstration purposes, was on the right. Pictures of Army hospitals, medics attending injured G.I.s, and ambulances used in the war hung on portable display walls. Shelving held James's collection of itchy green wool blankets, a folded pup tent that still smelled of insect repellant from the Pacific-front he had borrowed from his son Howard, G.I. field clothing, and a package of K-Rations* consisting of pemmican biscuits*, a peanut bar, raisins, and bouillon paste. A display of canteens was on a lower shelf. Tucker figured Uncle James put them there so active children couldn't break them if bumped off. The largest compilation was his many field-used surgical instruments he had acquired from friends who served in the medical corps. The other two tents on the courthouse lawn contained large collections of other objects from veterans or scout masters for their demonstrations.

Christy wandered from picture to picture. "Unbelievable," she whispered.

"Believe it," James said as he continued preparing for the people who would come in very soon. "Many lived it. They were there." He pointed to a large panorama* of the men landing in Normandy on D-Day. "It was the medic's job to stitch up as many of the injured as he could."

"Roger, that," she agreed, but shook her head in amazement at the same time.

"Sit, sit," Uncle James prompted Tucker with a tug on his sleeve. He pulled out a box from a drawer in the platform, placed it beside Tuck and opened the lid. "Now, first I'm going to put warm wax on your leg and quickly shape it to look like part of your own limb."

"Sure," Tucker agreed. "It's not real hot is it?" He paid little attention to whether something was dangerous, but had no interest in burning himself on wax. Gramma sealed all her quart canning jars with hot paraffin, and he knew that stuff could burn. He trusted just about everybody so he rolled up his pant leg and let his uncle apply the wax.

"Not hot, just warm." Uncle James smoothed it on, making sure it contoured to the boy's leg exactly. He used surgical tape to attach the bulb end of a long tube under Tucker's arm. The other end, he fed down through Tuck's pants leg and then under the wax. Uncle James drew the shape of a deep wound onto the wax and colored it with a squirt from the bulb filled with red liquid just as the first of the observers entered the tent.

"Oh my, young man," a lady in a flowered sundress, white gloves and sandals came in with her silent husband. She gasped as she approached Tucker on the cot. "How did that happen?"

Tucker smiled as the lady bent near to inspect the realistic-looking gash. She smelled like Carolyn's prized dark blue bottle of cologne called *Evening in Paris.*

It was time for the others to come in. "It really hurts," Tucker moaned with pain-filled eyes. "I fell down a little while ago."

"It was awful," Christy joined in the act. "We had just run across the street when a roly poly shaped guy, running from the other direction, plowed into him. Tucker flew up in the air and came down on the concrete sidewalk on the side of his leg." She looked at Tucker and shook her head. "Yep, it was sure awful."

"Indeed," the lady sighed. "You poor thing." The lady's face drew up tight while she made sure her white gloves didn't touch anything.

"Come on in folks." James stood back and made space for all the other spectators who wanted to see the demonstration of field treatment for injured G.I.s. He stepped to the side so as not to block Tucker's next lines in his "poor me" saga*.

Making sure no one saw him, Tucker pumped his arm again. Red *blood* oozed from the creative wound.

"Hurry, Mister." Glove-lady anxiously tapped on James's shoulder with her index finger. "Wayne," she told her husband, "he's bleeding so much." She buried her head on her husband's shoulder.

"Thank you, Ma'am." James opened the kit he had placed on the cot and took out a package of catgut sutures attached to semicircular surgical needles. "In order to help this boy by stitching up his cut," James explained, "I'll put on surgical gloves as they did on the war front. This will keep infection from the wound. Then, I'll take as many stitches as the cut requires."

The white-gloved lady smiled a little and leaned closer to the demonstration. "Now Dearie, you just remain calm."

"I am calm." Tucker released another squirt of the fake blood. "Wow, that one was juicy."

The lady gaged, grabbing her husband's arm as she started to swoon. "Oh hurry, hurry. He'll bleed to death before you get around to helping him."

"Quick, Mr. Moyer." Christy's over-dramatic voice sounded full of panic as she sat on the cot and put her arm around Tucker's shoulder. "What would his grandmother do if he couldn't walk again?" She grabbed Tucker's hand and held on.

"I'll fix him up." James assured her. First, he poured water from a brown hydrogen peroxide bottle that masqueraded* as antiseptic. Then, he stuck the threaded needle through the wax and into the other side of the gaping pretend gash, pulling the two sides together. The bogus*wound required seven stitches.

"There," James concluded. "The medics had to make sure all was as clean as possible in the grass and dirt, or the sands of Utah Beach."

"There Dearie," the lady removed her right glove and tapped Tucker on the shoulder. "Now, you're on the mend."

"Yes, Ma'am, thank you." Tucker smiled a silly smile and then pushed the bulb under his armpit again. Red fluid oozed out between the stitches and trickled down his leg.

"Oh no," the woman gasped. "The peroxide didn't fizz, Mr. Moyer. It wasn't any good."

"Hurry," Christy pleaded. "Mr. Moyer, he's bleeding again." She covered her eyes with her hands and peaked through her fingers.

James began putting the surgical equipment away. Then, he turned and nodded to Tucker.

"Don't worry, Ma'am," Tucker said with a smile and a giggle. "It's just part of the demonstration." He pulled up the edge of the wax that was tucked under the lower edge of his pant leg, just below his knee. "It's fake." He tried to be as serious and sympathetic as he could. While at the same time, inside, he had a great laugh about how well he acted out his part.

"Fake?" The woman's eyes bulged as she threw her hands to her face, smearing her bright red lipstick all over her mouth and staining both white gloves. "Well, of all the tricks. I never ..."

"Now, Velma," Wayne comforted his wife. "You never what? You've played in the little theater productions of many plays over the years. That was the boy's job, to fool everyone so the demonstration would appear real." He winked at Tucker. "You did a fine job."

"Thanks," Tucker smiled but didn't say more. He liked playing the part. Then he realized he liked even better tricking the lady into believing that he was actually hurt. He remembered what Gramma had said. Did he like the play-acting because it allowed him to stretch the facts just to scare people? Well... maybe.

Chapter 7
Early Sunday Morning

"I've called those two several times," Gramma sighed as she walked down the steps on Sunday morning, holding on to the banister.

Tucker was close behind. When he came to the landing and turned to go down the remaining steps, he threw his left leg over the banister and slid off onto the entry floor below.

Sparkling colors danced on the hardwood floor in the front hall at the bottom of the stairs. The kaleidoscope of color, created by the sun shining through prisms in the beveled edges of the glass in the front door, seemed to bless the house.

Gramma walked out into the kitchen, adjusting her belt as she went. "Here, let me get the eye dropper."

Tucker snickered to himself. He liked Gramma's kind of wake-up call … when applied to someone else. "Are Betsy and Tim still in bed?"

"Ja, Tucker, they are. Carolyn was up early. She's working this morning over at the telephone office."

The area telephone station was just across the street, behind the church parking lot. The operator managed a switchboard* where many party lines* connected phones in the area. If someone wanted to call a friend on the party line, they would take down the candlestick shaped receiver from the box that hung on the wall. With the receiver to their ear, they'd listen. If no one was talking and the line was clear, they'd hang up and dial the correct number of long and short sounds by turning the crank on the side of the box. If the person they wanted to call wasn't on the same party line, they'd dial the operator at the telephone office and ask them to place the call. The operator would plug one end of the line into the appropriate spot on their switchboard to connect the caller with a different exchange.

"I thought Carolyn wasn't supposed to work on Sundays," Tucker said as he followed his grandmother into the kitchen.

Gramma reached up on the small shelf on the wall near the side door and took down her blue hat with the little white daisy. "Dalia's daughter is sick with Scarlet Fever. The child has to stay in bed or she could become even sicker. Carolyn might have to work all week, not just on Saturday like regular." She put the hat on her head and stuck a hatpin through the back to hold it from slipping.

As Gramma picked up her music from the piano and placed it on the dining room table, Tucker stuck his finger in the jar of homemade grape jelly that sat open on the kitchen counter. He licked the sweet/tart jelly off his finger then reached again for the small fruit jar.

"No, Tucker. Keep your fingers out of the jam. Your grandfather got it out when he made the coffee. That's for your toast if you have time to eat some breakfast." Gramma reached into the cabinet that held her first aid supplies and took out an eye dropper she still had from putting drops in Grandpop's eye many years ago.

During Joseph Moyer's working years on the railroad, safety was always an issue. One hard day at work, a steel bar hit him in the eye, blinding him, retiring him, and requiring daily eye drops in that eye.

"Here," Gramma offered the dropper to Tucker. "Drop a little water on Tim's nose. He'll wake up then." Her smile told Tucker that Gramma was having fun. "Be sure to step out of the way, especially when you get to Betsy. She might wake up fighting. While you go upstairs with our wakeup call, I'll make sure we have the eggs and sugar for your tapioca later today. We can borrow some if necessary."

Tucker took the eyedropper and a small glass of water. Bounding back up the steps, two at a time, he thought … *This is gonna be fun.*

Tim's room was the small one at the end of the hall. He always slept with the door closed, regardless of how hot it was outside. Tucker twisted the door knob a full turn opening the door without a sound. Several pair of Tim's jeans lay on the floor, along with a couple of summer plaid shirts. A half-eaten apple, a revolting shade of brown was on the small bedside table. Tucker snuck quietly over to the bed, tipped the pointy end of the glass tube into the water filling it half-way, and carefully let a small dab drop on his brother's nose – then hopped back.

Sputtering and sneezing, Tim sat straight up, wiping his nose on the sheet. "Hey, Tucker. What ya think you're doing?"

"I'm Gramma's alarm clock," Tucker laughed as he slipped while hopping over Tim's dirty clothes. Balancing himself with the knuckles of one hand, he pushed himself back off the dresser. "It's time to get up for church." Tim was still sending choice words in his brother's direction when Tucker ran out of the room and down the hall.

Betsy and Carolyn shared a room at the other end of the hall. Tucker twisted around and burst through the door.

"Oh, no you don't," Betsy yelled. She covered her head with the baseball cap she snatched off the floor. "I heard you coming."

"Well … get up then." Tucker started to back out of the room and banged into the dresser. Without a blink or a "Sorry," he turned and skipped back down the steps looking for breakfast.

In the kitchen, Tucker dropped two pieces of Gramma's home-made bread in her new, chrome-plated, Sunbeam electric toaster. Uncle Jacob had bought it for her in celebration of her birthday in March. When the toast was a golden brown and the nutty smell filled the house, Tucker slathered on some of the jelly he had sampled earlier.

"Okay, I'm ready." Tim walked into the kitchen pulling a short-sleeve, navy blue shirt over his head.

"Be sure to comb your hair." Gramma patted his shoulder. "And, Tucker, what about Betsy?" Gramma smiled as Joseph came into the small kitchen. Although it was July, Grandpop had on a white shirt and his gray suit. She straightened his tie and touched his cheek.

Tucker noticed that his grandparents rarely kissed each other when he and the others were around. He guessed all married people stopped kissing each other when they got married. He figured it had something to do with being too tired. He recognized exhaustion in every wrinkle of Gramma's face at the end of each day.

Dressed in a tan cotton twill skirt with loops for a patent leather belt, and a red top, Betsy started out the side door. "Present and accounted for." She let the door bang behind her and hit her on the back of her new saddle shoes. The muddy spots where Tiny jumped up and scratched at the screen door smudged the back of her white bobby socks. She ran down the steps. "See ya at church."

Tucker glared at the back of his sister's dark brown ponytail and mumbled. *Betsy didn't even get up until I came into her room a few minutes ago. She's not getting there first,* he grumbled inside. With a leap from the side porch four steps down to the ground, he overtook Betsy before she got to the church parking lot. "Bye," he called out as he passed her. "See ya later."

Chapter 8
The Music of Sunday

Tucker jerked the church door open, dashed inside, then slowed to a respectful walk. His Sunday shoes clicked on the tile under his feet. Down the hall and around the corner to the left, Tucker pushed on the swinging doors that led into the sanctuary*. Even though the alter candles were not yet lit, he could smell the aroma of the wax.

Freddie walked up the center aisle behind him, not running, just using long strides. "Come on, Tucker. Let's sit in the balcony."

"Sure," Tucker agreed with outward enthusiasm. But that Sunday, he wasn't sure about sitting with the other kids.

The rest of the family entered the sanctuary and scattered. Gramma went up to the front of the church and sat down at the pump organ*. Tucker knew that music was one of her passions. As she got older, he wondered if things might have to change. At seventy-seven, his grandmother was either going to have to stop playing the organ with its two hard pushing pump peddles near the floor, or the church was going to have to buy a newer model. Pumping through the opening music, then four hymns, and the closing accompaniment was almost impossible for her weary legs. Running a musical marathon was now beyond her ability.

Tucker was always vigilant. He saw Betsy's red shirt slip into the nursery to help with the toddlers. He had often watched as she got down on the floor with the little ones and crawled around. He could see how much the children loved her. Tucker knew that Betsy never told Gramma that she wore shorts under her skirt. To his way of thinking, shorts under his sister's clothes made more sense than Betsy's underpants shining in the church.

Two large bouquets in cut-glass vases graced the alter table. Red roses, blue carnations and white daisies clustered with large white lilies and baby's breath. Tucker inhaled the beauty and the sweetness. He thought of Gramma's flower beds on the north side of the front yard and smiled.

Johnny Washington came in and looked around. "There you are," he called across the sanctuary.

"I'm glad you came, Johnny. A bunch of us are going upstairs to sit in the balcony." Tucker motioned for him to follow. "Come on."

Johnny looked over at the choir members who had followed him into the sanctuary and asked in a general anyone-can-answer mode, "Is it okay if I sit up top with Tucker?"

A man with a deep base voice and an alto-sounding lady spoke at the same time. "Sure Johnny."

Tucker and Johnny followed Freddie to the back of the church where they took the side stairs to the balcony. However, Tucker felt odd. Rather than feeling free to be with his friends, his feet seemed heavier with each step he took, even though he wasn't wearing his clodhoppers. *What's wrong with me?*

"Good morning, Tuck," Christy greeted with a smile as she brushed back her hair. Several other girls from school clustered around her on the front pew. "Hi Johnny," Christy added when she saw him behind Tucker. She scooted over, making sure there would be room on the pew beside her for all three boys.

"This is Johnny Washington," Tucker told the gaggle of female geese that had already flocked there.

The girls smiled and nodded. Each went on talking, one phrase buried under the partial sentence of the previous girl and then the next.

Tucker watched and half-way listened as each girl seemed to compete to be the center of attention. All Tucker heard was the same *cackle* they usually seemed to quack.

"Sounds like you might have something to say," he said as he laughed. "If your giggles didn't sound like cackles."

"Okay, fly boy," Anna Fredrick sassed. "If you hadn't gotten your ears stuffed up while you were up in the clouds in your flying hammock, you could understand us."

"If you had something worth listening to, I'd listen closer," Tucker snapped back with an infectious grin.

Christy reached over and tapped him on the arm. "I personally stood under the P-51 he strung up there, and I wished I could have gone up. Might have been like piloting the B-36 that flew over."

Anna turned up her nose. "Need a girl to help you out, Mr. Lindberg?"

"No," Tucker put his hands in his church pants pockets and rocked back and forth. "Next time I go flying, you want to ride along? Or, are you afraid?"

"No," Anna sputtered. "Next time you fly a hammock, I'll go along."

Freddie snickered. "That hammock was only twenty feet off the ground. I'm sure that wouldn't be too high for you."

Anna swallowed hard. "Twenty feet? Sure … that's not too high. Besides, it's not the height … it's the toes-over-teakettle on the way down I wouldn't like."

"Right," Tucker cracked. He turned to Christy. "Why don't you and I, Freddie and Johnny go down and sit with Grandpop?"

Anna smiled a crooked smile. "What's the matter? Can't take the brilliance up here?"

"Don't worry about it, Anna." Tucker turned to leave. "I know hot air rises."

Freddie got in step behind Christy who followed Tucker. "Sounds good to me." Johnny was close behind. He covered his mouth to muffle a laugh.

As Tucker and his friends emerged from the stairs, Joseph came through the double doors at the back of the church.

"Had a talk with a member of the Trustees," he said as his deep voice rumbled around him. "He asked me what I thought about the Youth using that large room down in the basement. The one you enter before you get to the boiler room. Ping pong tables and a couple of shuffle board courts are already set up. They fit fine. It's a big space."

"That would be great, Mr. Moyer," Freddie and Christy chimed in together.

"When will it be ready?" Tucker asked as he stepped back to let the three friends enter the pew before him and his grandfather. Grandpop always sat at the end where he could rest on the back of the pew and use the end support as an armrest.

"When? The stuff is there. The trustee thought it would be nice if you kids put a new coat of paint on the walls." Grandpop threw his head back with satisfaction.

Tucker couldn't believe it. He and his friends had asked for a place to hang out for a long time. The high school kids pushed the hardest, but Pastor Daily had insisted that any space they found had to be open to all the children of the church. "Maybe we can set up a schedule," Tucker brainstormed. "When the senior high can use it and another time for the junior high."

"You'll work out all the details," Grandpop settled the issue as Gramma began to play the introit*. He settled back into his usual comfortable position.

The choir loft burst with singers. With the addition of the A.M.E. songsters, the beams in the ceiling seemed to echo. As Pastor Daily directed everyone to stand up, Tucker heard his grandmother play a few bars of the music and then the first hymn began. The musical sound that burst forth resonated in Tucker's heart.

Setting beside Tucker, his grandfather still towered over him. In recent years, his six feet height withered a little. But to Tucker, Grandpop was a big man. Regardless of how much he would shrink and Tucker would grow, Grandpop would always be a tower of strength.

"Here ya go, Grandpop." Luke, Aunt Cora and Uncle Jerry's son, was an usher that morning, passing out the bulletins. Luke smiled at his cousin.

Tucker nodded but had nothing to say. He thought about what his grandmother had said. "Cousins are everywhere." But Tucker wanted more.

For now, he would settle for the sound of Grandpop's deep voice as he sang *Amazing Grace,* the song Gramma was practicing yesterday. When his grandfather's bass voice joined in with the sound of the two choirs, the mellow music soothed Tucker's ears and set the wooden pew vibrating.

Toward the end of the service, everyone stood again as the introductory bars of the *Star-Spangled Banner* filled the cathedral-ceiling. The windows of the large sanctuary were open letting in a breeze that rustled the American flag in its stand.

Thrilled by the music and soft breath of wind, Tucker's sense of patriotism gave him a strange feeling in his throat. *I am not going to cry,* he insisted to himself. Christy tapped Tucker on the sleeve, nudged toward Joseph and smiled. Tucker leaned the backs of his knees against the wooden pew and felt the music move through his muscles. It was a good start to a Sunday morning.

Chapter 9
Birdie Kline

After the church service, Birdie Kline tried to round up her Junior High Sunday school class as they drifted in and out of the classroom. "Okay, everybody," she said as she herded the students into one well-knit group.

Tucker was amazed how Mrs. Kline could keep the class from scaling the walls and still come off as a calm, Christian woman…at least most Sundays. One Sunday, Tucker heard her tell Pastor Dailey she failed to see how some acts of adolescents* were "Christian." She considered Junior High kids as inhabitants from another planet who didn't use Earth-speak.

"It's hot in here," Anna complained as she cooled her face with the church bulletin she had folded back and forth, accordion pleating it, into an ideal shape for fanning.

"Well, let's all sit down," Birdie encouraged.

Anna plopped down on a slatted wooden folding chair she had scooted as close to the open window as possible. "Woe is me," she sighed loudly.

"Miss Woe is at it again," Tucker teased as he picked at the candle wax that gathered in small puddles on the dish beneath the unlit taper. The wax felt the same as that which Gramma had used to make Christmas candles, but with a little fragrance added. He rolled the small pieces between his fingers, creating larger balls, and then secretly popped them at Anna and others in the class. The candle drippings he picked at were the half-burnt red pieces from February. It smelled like rose water. Mrs. Cooper had made those candles for Valentine's Day gifts and placed several in the church.

With her wonderful thick sliced homemade bread and cherry pies, all Mrs. Cooper needed was a meat product to complete her desire to be a butcher, a baker, and a candle stick maker.

"Don't call me Miss Woe," Anna demanded with a whine in her voice. "Mrs. Kline, make him stop."

Freddie's face turned red, which wasn't hard for a red head. If Tucker didn't know better, he would swear, if Gramma allowed him to swear anything, that Freddie liked Anna Fredrick.

Tucker shook off that thought for fear he may have discovered a truth that was too awful to think about. Just imagine holding hands with a girl who had her nose so high in the air she wouldn't be able to see who was around her. He quickly changed the subject.

"Mrs. Kline," Tucker turned to Johnny, "this is Johnny Washington, the choir director's son."

"Goldie's boy?" Birdie reached out to Johnny with a hug. "I grew up in Elkhart, Johnny. I went to school with your mama."

"You did?" Johnny questioned with large eyes.

Birdie's face danced with what looked like happy memories. "I was a year ahead of her, but we both sang in the school choir and had some classes together."

"That's nice, Mrs. Kline." Johnny said with a broad smile. "Mama talks a lot about singing in the choir in high school."

"Yvonne," Anna whined to the girl at her side. "Quit pushing."

Yvonne Sherbet was about six inches shorter than the shortest class member, and many pounds less. "I'm not pushing, Anna. You're blocking the breeze."

"Am not," Anna moaned.

"Are too," Yvonne snapped over the top of Anna's *am-not*.

Christy rolled her eyes and sat down beside Tucker. She didn't need to draw attention to herself. Her whisper to

Tucker was enough. "Am-not and are-too want to be the center of attention. Maybe the Bible lesson should be about them."

"Bible lesson? No," Tucker sighed deeply and shook his head as he remembered a book Uncle Jacob had read to Betsy and him when they were little. "It needs to be a lesson from Dr. Dolittle where a pushmi-pullyu, a two headed animal, can eat with one head while talking with the other. That way he can't interrupt if his other end is talking…only when it's his turn while the other head is eating."

Christy wrinkled up her nose. "What did you just say?"

"Hey, I know," Tucker ignored the question as he whipped around excitedly, always looking for a way to stop an argument. "Mrs. Kline, can we have our class outside, under that big tree beside the door?"

"Yes," Johnny said as he wiped his forehead with his white handkerchief. "This is the day for breeze and shade."

"That sounds like a good idea," Birdie answered as she looked around at the very active kids.

That morning, the lesson was supposed to be Daniel in the Lion's Den, but the way it was unfolding Tucker didn't see how that was going to be possible. "Maybe we can learn about Zacchaeus," he suggested. "We'll have a tree right there as exhibit number one."

"Another good idea," Birdie agreed. "Okay. Gilbert, Raymond, Ralph, all of you, grab a folding chair, walk, don't run outside. Stay together."

Outside, a breeze made the temperature feel ten degrees cooler. A bed of Lily of the Valley Aunt Cora had planted next to the church sent floral perfume into the air. The class unfolded their chairs and sat in a semi-circle.

As Birdie sat in the chair Gilbert had carried for her, she placed a small picnic basket that hung from her arm onto her lap. "Thank you for being quiet," she told the class before they could start another conversation or argument.

"Gilbert, will you and Darla pass out the brownies and a napkin to put them on."

"Brownies?" Tucker called out. "I'll help pass them around."

"Thank you Tucker," Birdie said with a broad smile. "Gilbert and Darla are helping right now."

When the basket and napkins got to Tucker, he saw there was only one left. As good as it looked, thick and soft and smelled like sweet cocoa, he was glad the last one appeared to be the largest. If he were at home, he would also gather up the many crumbs that dotted the bottom of the plate inside.

"Sorry, Mrs. Kline, this is the last one." Tucker took a bite and held the dark chocolatey goodness in his mouth.

"I know," she laughed. "The truth is I had a brownie earlier this morning when I made them. Plus, I saved several for our dessert after lunch. My second brownie is waiting for me at home, all stacked up with the others in my cookie jar."

For the first time since the kids gathered for class, it was quiet. Full mouths are quiet mouths. Christy took another bite and whispered, "Maybe there won't be time for a Bible lesson."

"I heard that Christy." Birdie corrected as she sat the basket on the grass. "We'll have a very short lesson."

"Yeah!" Several of the class cheered.

"I like your idea about studying Zacchaeus, Tucker," Birdie said with a smile. "Remember, Zacchaeus was a short man. Jesus's appearances drew huge crowds by that time in his ministry. Zacchaeus wouldn't be able to see Jesus as he walked by unless he climbed the tree. He couldn't expect anyone to help him get a better look because he had few friends. People didn't drop by his home, or start up a conversation with him on the streets. The little man was a tax collector, and people didn't like tax collectors. When Jesus came down the road, he stopped at the base of the tree

Zacchaeus had climbed. He told him to get down because he was going to go to his house for dinner."

"So, even if no one likes you," Tucker thought it through, "Jesus will still be your friend."

Mrs. Kline stared at him, stunned until she found her words. "That's exactly right, Tucker."

Tucker hadn't taken his eyes off Mrs. Kline's basket. He could almost taste each of the many brownie crumbs the basket still held. As he watched the woven brownie-holder he grinned at one point but no one noticed. He saw something no one else saw. Without thinking, as usual, he concluded, "That means … even Anna has a friend in Jesus."

"What?" Anna barked. "Are you saying no one else likes me?"

"No…" Birdie drew out lovingly while shooting a bewildered look at Tucker. "It means Jesus loves you …just like he loves everyone."

Johnny sat speechless. The Sunday school class he attended at his church was nothing like this one. His eyes danced as he watched the confusion.

Freddie shot a glance at Tucker then back to the others. He wiggled uncomfortably and finally blurted out. "I'll be your friend, Anna."

"But …" Anna began then stopped. A tiny softening spread across her lips. "That's nice, Freddie."

"Well," Christy's eyes seemed to search the group for words. "It looks like the story of Zacchaeus has many examples."

Tucker reached for the picnic basket. Did he think first? No. In fact, he didn't think at all. He simply found something special and the rest of the story just tumbled out in front of him. "We could have talked about Adam and Eve this morning, Mrs. Kline." His hand quickly slipped into her picnic basket. "I have an example for that one, too." He reached in the open hamper and pulled out the garter snake he had seen slither into the basket just minutes before. "The snake tempted Eve, and… here it is!" He danced around the yard with the wiggly reptile pinched between his fingers. Its yellow beady eyes flashed and its forked tongue spit out as the kids scrambled under that tree.

"No," Anna yelled, burying her face in her hands. "Keep it away from me."

At that moment, no one was on Tucker's side. In his usual fun, he didn't even notice that none of the kids were smiling with him.

"Put that thing down, Tucker McBride," Birdie ordered. "I'll go get your grandfather. He'll not think this is so funny."

"Sure he would. He likes snakes," Tucker laughed. He dangled the tan, earthy, three foot long snake in the air. When he lowered it to taunt Yvonne, Christy stepped in between her and the serpent with the green stripe.

"Give me that thing, Tucker McBride." Christy whispered gruffly as she grabbed the snake in her fist. She marched over to the flower bed several yards away and flung the thing onto the ground.

Tucker's huge eyes glistened with amazement. "Wow!"

Chapter 10
Secrets

Tucker flipped himself up into the tree they had just had class under and hung upside down from the lowest branch. From there, he could watch others streaming out of the church without seeming to stalk the congregation. He began to doubt the wisdom of his prank with the snake. He hoped to run interference between Mrs. Kline and his grandfather. When Grandpop came out into the sunlight, Tucker saw Christy go over to Birdie and show her an imaginary sliver buried in the heel of her hand. He smiled. Christy was covering for him again.

Tucker darted across the street and stood on the side porch of the house, watching the people as they left. He saw Birdie Kline turn toward Grandpop just as Christy moaned and gripped her hand even more tightly. Grandpop kept walking toward the house, paying no attention to the injured Christy Tree. "Thanks Christy," Tucker whispered.

Inside the house, the family was abuzz with meal preparation. Aunt Cora, Uncle Jerry and Luke always came over after church. It was a true family dinner. Cora would send Jerry home for the hot and creamy scalloped potatoes she had waiting in the oven on warm. The green beans were in a large pan on the back burner of Gramma's old wood stove where they had cooked on low all morning. The Lehman house was only a short block down Meir Street that ran behind the Moyer house. Gramma supplied the browned roast, the home made yeasty bread, and one of her daily pies. Tucker had no real favorite. The pumpkin with mounds of whipping cream his grandmother had selected for that day would settle his taste just fine. He loved pie…any pie.

As the table began to fill with the usual Sunday meal dishes, Tucker darted up the steps.

"Look out, Tucker. I'm coming through," Betsy pushed her way past him, taking two steps at a time.

Tucker slipped into his room, took off his dress pants and hung them carefully on a pants hanger, then threw his shirt over it too. Grabbing his jeans from a corner of the floor and a fresh shirt from the drawer, in order to smell clean at the Sunday dinner table, he knelt down and pulled his clodhoppers from under the bed. His shoes were only half tied, but that was good enough. He didn't want to be out of his seat when any of the serving dishes passed by.

Downstairs, the whole family gathered around the table. Betsy had changed her clothes and wiggled into her chair just after Tucker sat down. Before a spoon or fork touched any mouth, they bowed their heads so Grandpop could say grace. He thanked God for the food He had provided, and for the loving hands that prepared it. "And, Lord," Grandpop concluded, "thank you for Tucker. He makes us stay young, and causes the young to grow up so they can outrun him and any reptile he may be holding. Amen."

Tucker was shocked. So, Grandpop did know about the garter snake. Still, his grandfather hadn't bawled him out. He hadn't even spoken to him directly about it. Grandpop had found a way to talk to him through God himself.

While Cora passed Jerry the meat platter, Uncle Jerry asked, "Anyone hear about that snake today over at the church?"

"What snake?" Betsy asked as she popped to attention.

Tucker brought a forkful of potatoes to his mouth, stuffing it so full be couldn't say anything.

Aunt Cora sighed as she placed a small piece of roast on her plate. "I heard there was one in the church yard."

Gramma spooned some bacon and onion flavored green beans onto her plate. "Birdie Kline said she saw it."

Tucker coughed and nearly choked.

Betsy jerked his hand up over his head as he came up for air. "You okay?"

"Yep," he wheezed. When he cleared his throat enough to talk, he continued to stare at the food on his plate and asked, "Did she say anything else about it?" Then he thought he'd better cover his question. "Thought I might look for it and bring it home."

Gramma jumped as her fork clattered to her plate. "Tucker McBride, don't you dare bring a snake into this house."

"Yes, Ma'am," he said, putting on a great pretense of disappointment. Secretly, he was glad the topic of snakes was by-passed.

"Let's change the subject," Gramma sighed deeply, fanning herself with the hem of her apron. "Umm, does the pie meet with your approval, Tucker?" She asked with a wink.

"Twice the size would have been better," he said with a grin.

"Pure boy," Grandpop teased.

By the time they all cleared the dinner dishes, Tucker was full. He knew he'd stay full for the next few hours until hunger took over again. Then pudding would solve the hunger pains.

Every Sunday afternoon, it was his pleasure to make a triple recipe of tapioca for an afternoon snack. It was too early for the creamy pudding at that point. Now what was he going to do?

Luke excused himself with a cheerful, "Great dinner, Grandma. I promised to meet a friend at the library." He kissed his mother on the forehead and left.

Tucker watched Luke go and wondered if he'd be able to slip away that easily on a Sunday afternoon when he was a few years older. Gramma preferred everyone rest on the Sabbath. Only a few activities met with her approval. Taking an afternoon stroll was on her list of acceptable relaxing activities.

"Tucker," Betsy poked him on the shoulder as she put her plate on the stack of dishes on the kitchen counter. "I'm going for a walk. Want to come along?"

"Sure," Tucker said but wondered what this walk was all about. Still, he would be *doing,* so he fell in behind her as they darted out the door. "See ya later," he called when the screen door banged.

Chapter 11
The Sunday Afternoon Game

Tucker and Betsy took giant strides as they walked around the side of the house and back through the yard to the alley gate. Tucker was competitive* in every little part of his life. He picked up speed and began to race Betsy to the vacant lot where Freddie, Christy, and several other guys from the neighborhood had already gathered.

"Where's your ball glove?" Christy called out.

Tucker shrugged. He was unwilling to admit he didn't want to go up to his room to get the glove out of his closet and then have to walk through the house with it in his hand. "Couldn't get to it," was his excuse.

Betsy laughed, reached into the bushes at the border of the lot and pulled out two Rawlings mitts. "I stashed them in here when you were in Goshen yesterday."

"Thanks!" Tucker thankfully took the mitt, put it on and drove his fist into the leather in the palm.

As they got organized, the friends chose-up sides and positions. Tucker was the catcher for his team. The sun was beating down as the game moved through the first three innings. Play after play: runs, hits, and stolen bases, progressed the game at a fast pace. Betsy, of course, hit the only home run so far, driving the ball past the outfield boundary. She could beat any player.

Tucker, strong and agile*, came to bat again. He hit the second pitch so far into the outfield, fielders had to run backwards to try to catch it. Mrs. Honeycutt's big weeping willow tree was the far boundary for the field.

As Tucker raced around the bases, first, second, third … home was all that remained for a win for his team. Just a few more yards … then he hit the ground and slid into the plate, hands first. Carl Daniels was pitching. When Tucker passed Betsy at third base, she threw the ball back to the pitcher. Carl slammed the hard ball into home plate just as Tucker stood up laughing.

Everyone let out a gasp that seemed to suck all the air out of the sandlot. Immediately, Tucker spun around as the baseball crashed into the side of his head. He hit the ground with a thud as dust scattered everywhere. Half conscious*, half not, he saw stars swirl around his head, like bees swarming above him. To Tucker, they seemed to buzz through his ears and pop out on the other side of his head.

Since Christy was next-up, she was near the batter's box. Throwing her bat to the side, she dove to home plate. "Tucker, are you okay?" She grabbed his arm and tried to pull him up.

Betsy screamed and scrambled over from her position. "Let him be," she ordered. "Let him catch his breath." When she got closer, her expression became serious. "Tucker, are you hurt?"

Tucker never admitted injury, so his response was the same as always. "I'm okay." He didn't try to sit up. He stayed in the dirt for another few minutes and then leaned up on one elbow. He stopped there. At first he thought he was going to throw up as his world kept spinning. It sounded like a flock of birds was preforming a concerto* in a high pitched bell-choir between his ears.

"Sorry I yelled, Christy." Betsy's breath was short; her hand trembled with anxiety. She always stuck up for her little brother. "Help me get him up." With Betsy on one arm and Christy on the other, they helped him stand.

Tucker gagged in deep dry heaves, trying to force his dinner to stay down. He hated the after taste of passing his meal through his mouth twice.

"Christy, help me get him home." Betsy tried to support her brother under his arm. Tucker wiggled himself free, pulling away.

"I can walk by myself." he insisted. He was perfectly capable of taking care of himself. *Independent* was his middle name. In an after-thought, he quickly found straightening his body was hard to do.

Christy's brow creased in worry. "We'll walk along with you anyway and carry your ball glove. I'll need to check in at home in a little bit."

"I don't want to worry Gramma and Grandpop," he assured her. The sound of his own voice seemed muffled in his ears.

"No one needs to know about the ball game on Sunday or the smack in the head," Betsy agreed.

Tucker knew he could trust his sister. Together they had bounced around the neighborhood for years, always coming home in time for supper. The world within walking distance around them was their own personal playground.

Every step Tucker took felt like hammers were pounding on his head. The pressure rattled all the way down to his stomach.

When the three reached the Moyer house, Betsy opened the back, summer house door. As quietly as they could with a wobbly banged-up Tucker in tow, they stepped inside and listened to the house. Tucker paused and looked at the two girls. None of them said anything, but he knew they understood.

Betsy tapped Christy on the shoulder, took Tuck's ball glove from her, and slipped over to the left. Waving the two gloves at Tucker, she stuffed them into the oven of the old cast iron stove. Tucker nodded in agreement.

He whispered as Betsy came back to the landing where they'd either go down to the basement or up to the kitchen. "Tomorrow is wash day. Grandpop will fire up the stove for hot water. Better get them out later."

"Right," she agreed as they walked into the kitchen.

"There you are." Gramma was just taking afternoon coffee into the dining room when the three came in. She stopped in mid-stride when she saw their condition. "What on earth happened to you three?"

Tucker dug deep to find a smile left inside before the Ted Williams meteor hit him on the head. "I'm okay," he offered as he looked around at double everything in the room. "I fell down." Nothing could have been truer.

Betsy laughed awkwardly. "Christy and I pulled him out of the dirt."

"Oh my," Gramma looked the three over, shaking her head. "Ja, I see. Well, go in and cleanup. You'll want to make tapioca pretty soon."

Tapioca was one of Tucker's favorite foods, but after his tangle with Carl's baseball, nothing sounded good. How was he going to make a big bowl full of it for everyone to share?

"In a little bit." Tucker stumbled into the small bathroom. The mirror on the medicine cabinet reflected four eyes and two noses. He took a washcloth from the rack and washed his face, careful not to pull the skin or twist his neck.

Gramma said that I shouldn't stretch the truth. Grandpop needed some days of peace. If I told her I may have a concussion, she might think that was an exaggeration, he reasoned with himself. *I'd be doing them both a favor if I don't give them all the details.* He dried his face on the small hand towel while looking in the mirror again. *No,* he answered himself, *I didn't lie about anything. I told the truth. I definitely fell down.*

Christy was still standing by the door when he came out. She looked at him but said nothing.

"Thanks, for your help, Christy," he said with a weak smile.

She smiled back, that knowing kind of smile that said, "I'm with you." She turned and reached for the door. "I'll see you later."

"I hope so." Tucker knew he was seeing double and hoped that would soon pass.

When Christy left, Tucker spread out on the living room floor in front of the radio. Aunt Cora and Uncle Jerry were drinking their coffee in the kind of silence that hangs in the air when family and friends see each other every day. Everyone had already talked about the important things in their lives.

Most Sundays, Tucker would have opened the colorful comics section of the newspaper by that time. He'd spread them out on the floor and hover over them on his hands and knees. Not that day.

Tiny was the only one that noticed Tucker had a terrible headache. She crept over to him on her tummy and curled up beside him with her head on his chest. Tucker closed his eyes and waited for the world to stop spinning.

Chapter 12
Double the Strings

Later that Sunday evening the habits of the house fell into place. Aunt Cora and Uncle Jerry had gone home. Tucker's head was feeling a little better. When the double vision passed, he sat up but wasn't ready to read.

Tim was out for food with his friends at Bowers Drive-In over in Goshen, the hot spot in the county. Tucker thought he could smell the double decker hamburgers with onion and cheese all the way to his house. Maybe he was finally getting hungry. Carolyn had a date, and Tucker imagined food was involved. Betsy had walked over to the church to join the youth group for shuffle board on the basement floor, chocolate chip cookies and punch.

Out in the kitchen, the bright red box of dry tapioca waited. He'd have to do something about that. Bending over to get a pan out of Gramma's cupboard made his head hurt, but he pushed himself anyway. He put the large sauce pan on the burner, and mixed the milk and eggs together until they were blended. Next, he stirred in some sugar and some of the dry tapioca. When he brought it all to a full boil, he had to stand there and stir it constantly even though he wanted to close his eyes again. Adding the wonderfully smelling vanilla was the last step before pouring it all into a large bowl. The aroma perked him up. Since the ice box* wasn't very large, he saw no point in chilling it. Besides, eating it while it was still hot was his favorite.

This needed to be a two course meal. Tucker pulled a large black pan from a lower cabinet. It had a domed lid with a crank on the top. From a can by the stove he spooned out a small blob of lard, dropped it into the pan, and turned on the gas. As the grease got hot, he removed the lid from the large can of popcorn Gramma kept on top of the ice box. When the corn began popping, he vigorously turned the crank on the top of the pan lid. After a few minutes, the popping slowed to a stop and he took it off the burner. Pouring the hot exploded corn into one of Gramma's large mixing bowls, he took some butter from the ice box, melted it, and poured it over the corn. With two of Gramma's wooden mixing spoons Grandpop had made, he mixed it all together as if he were tossing a salad.

Tucker took several small cereal bowls into the dining room and placed them on the table with a fist full of spoons. On one side of the table, he put the bowl of hot tapioca pudding and the buttery popcorn sat at the other end.

"Here it is," he called to the family, just as Uncle Jacob walked into the living room carrying his violin. Jacob placed the black leather case on the floor, lifted the two latches and removed the golden wood violin. When the bow was unclipped from its fixed spot, he positioned the violin under his chin.

Tucker's shoulders slumped when someone knocked on the door. He walked toward the porch, keeping his eye on the best food in the county. At least he thought it was. "I'll get it," he offered.

"Hi, Tucker." Christy stepped into the room as he held the door. "Our radio isn't working right," she whispered. "Do you think I could listen with you?"

Tucker felt his cheeks grow warm. He wondered if he were allergic to Christy. That hot reaction only happened when Christy was around. He knew he wasn't allergic to Rosie, Christy's potbelly pig. Then, he remembered Christy had a cat. Maybe that was it.

"Tucker?" Christy asked again.

"Sure," he said as he snapped back to the question. "Come on in." He tried to wipe off the silly grin he could feel spreading across his face. This was a different kind of visit. Christy usually came over in the daytime. "Gramma, is it all right if Christy listens to the radio here this evening? The pudding and popcorn are ready."

"Ja, sure," Gramma agreed as she looked up from her Bible reading. "I think you can hear the radio all right. Jacob will be playing his violin, too."

Christy smiled. "That would be great. Daddy told me Mr. Moyer plays the violin but I've never heard him." Leaning toward Tucker she whispered, "How do you feel?"

"Better," he said as he gave a positive nod.

Gramma answered as she glanced down again. "Christy, you are always welcome."

"Thank you, Mrs. Moyer." Christy watched as Tucker's grandma began reading. "Mrs. Moyer, what have you been reading about in your Bible?"

"Same as always, Christy," she said with a deep sigh. "The Good Book tells us how to rear up a child in the way he should go." Gramma looked at Tucker and winked. "I need help every day on that. And, once I figure it out, something else happens, and I have to go back to the Scriptures."

"Yes, Ma'am," Christy agreed and smiled at Tucker.

Gramma patted the old leather book and turned to Jacob. "Before you start, Jacob," she said as she put a small crocheted cross in her Bible and closed it, "I made a fresh pot of coffee. If you want a cup, you can bring one for me, too."

"Sounds gut to me," Grandpop joined in. He had a pencil in his hand with the Sunday newspaper turned to the crossword puzzle.

Tucker watched as his grandfather worked through the puzzle one clue at a time. He whispered to Christy, "Grandpop finishes the puzzle every Sunday." It was amazing to Tucker. How could a man of his age know all those words? But then, Tucker thought Grandpop could do anything. Crosswords were just one more accomplishment*.

"Coffee sounds great about now." Jacob looked over as Tiny came into the room. He put the violin and bow back into the safe case. "Tucker," he whispered. "How about helping me bring in three cups of java*?"

Tucker looked over at the radio. His program, *The Jack Benny Show* was ready to come on. If he hurried, he wouldn't miss any of it. Benny was a funny man with a rather sarcastic sense of humor. He said things Tucker wished he had thought of, but Gramma would have thought him sassy if he had spoken them aloud.

"Christy, you want to help?"

"Sure," she brightened. "There's always so much going on at your house. It's just Daddy, Momma and me at our house."

"Hadn't thought about that." Tucker had thought Christy's family would be a perfect set up, with both a mom and a dad at home.

Out in the kitchen, Uncle Jacob was taking cups and saucers out of the cabinet. Tucker grabbed up the coffee pot just as he heard the radio announcer, Don Wilson, from the other room.

"Tonight, Jack welcomes Phil Harris, Eddie 'Rochester' Anderson, and of course, the lovely Mary Livingston," Wilson announced in his deep, rumbling voice.

Tucker poured two cups. Christy carried one of them to Mrs. Moyer. Tuck brought in the other one for Grandpop. Uncle Jacob brought his own into the living room and placed it on the side table beside his chair.

"Gramma, the popcorn is on the table. I popped it before Christy got here. Do you want some?"

"No thank you, Tucker." Neither did his grandfather or Uncle Jacob at that time. Gramma added, "If we want some later, you can pop us some more."

"How about some tapioca?"

"I'll wait for it to cool and then serve myself. Thanks."

Tucker and Christy sat on the floor with the large bowl of buttered corn placed between them and two large servings of fluffy pudding.

The house was quiet, except for the soft sound of Jack Benny's off tune violin screeching in the background. Tucker was intently listening to the silly antics of the group of friends on the radio when he saw Uncle Jacob open the case, take out the violin and bow again, adding soothing music to the squawk of Mr. Benny's instrument.

Tucker looked down at his uncle's black violin case … and smiled.

Chapter 13
Monday Washday

Tucker got up early the next morning. He was amazed at how much better he felt. The double vision had passed, and he hoped the ear ringers would put away their bells soon. He was ready to start planning his day.

Downstairs, the living room danced with sunbeams that streamed through the window. The multi-colored flickering specks of refracted light made him smile. The radio seemed to be the point where the sun focused a spotlight to announce the beginning of the *Lone Ranger**. Tucker knew the masked man would be on much later that day. Since Christy's home radio wasn't working properly, maybe he'd better check the equipment at his house. He'd turn on the radio to see if Uncle Jerry had fixed it.

Jerry Lehman could fix or create anything electronic. Reared Amish, he went through the eighth grade of school. In the Amish tradition, with eighth grade graduation, he had completed all the schooling he would get. Still, Jerry wanted more. He read everything he could find, from Mathematics, to History, to Literature. What he couldn't get his fill of was all things electronic.

In spring planting seasons, walking behind a team of stout plow horses, his mind would wander from the simple life of plain living* to everything he read in the *Popular Mechanics*. Although sheltered from the ways of the world on the family farm, he wanted a college education.

Old-order Amish never drive cars, but that didn't stop Jerry. He borrowed an English neighbor's truck, drove over to South Bend and talked to an admissions officer about taking tests that would prove he already knew the stuff he would have learned if he'd gone to high school. After all, graduating from high school was a basic entrance requirement for Notre Dame University. He took the College Level Examination Program test for every class in high school and CLEPPED out of each one. Jerry's gifts and talents in electronics even landed him an invitation from one of his professors to teach some of the classes. Tucker had heard the family story of *Uncle Jerry at Notre Dame* often.

Gramma and Grandpop had gotten up when darkness still hid behind every tree. They had their breakfast of coffee and toast, and then Gramma settled in her rocker to read her Bible. Joseph pulled the pocket knife he had bought in town from his pocket, turning it over and over. He inspected every blade and file.

Once a month, Grandpop would walk across the street and wait for the Elkhart to Goshen bus. He'd ride into Goshen to bank his eighty dollar retirement check at the Salem Bank. From his deposit, he'd save out some money to go to a hardware store and buy a small hand tool, a pocket knife, or some new type of pliers. Sometimes he'd buy a fresh fish or some limburger cheese.

One hot July day, he bought limburger cheese, double wrapped in a newspaper. When the inner wrapper broke, the terrible odor of the cheese filled the bus. Other riders gagged from the smell and complained to the driver. They told him they wouldn't ride the bus again if Mr. Moyer was on it.

Later that day, the bus driver came by the Moyer house and talked to Gramma. "I'm sorry, Mrs. Moyer. I've asked your husband to not bring cheese or fish on the bus; but he did again today. If he continues to bring stinky food on the bus, I'll have to ban him from riding."

"Ja, I understand," Gramma said as she directed him to the door. Then, stopping, she added, "My husband is a very stubborn man."

"Yes, Ma'am," the driver said as he left.

Grandpop must have learned his lesson, because Tucker saw him, once again, inspecting a tool with great care. Later, he'd take it out to his workshop and put it safely in a chest. Tucker figured Grandpop must have agreed. Cheese and fish would have to come home with Uncle Jacob.

With a knock on the screen door, Tucker hurried over. "I'll get it." He could see a man in a round black hat and black suit made of coarse fabric, with a large blue bib apron over the top, standing there with his hand on the door latch.

"Morning, Tucker," the man said as he opened the door.

Tucker paused to get a good look at Roman Swartz's horse as it stood hitched to an Amish delivery wagon, lined in sawdust and straw for hauling ice. Tucker loved horses, and those hitched to a buggy of any kind were much more graceful than the plow horses.

"Good morning, Roman." Tucker followed the man as he entered the house carrying a huge block of ice, about one foot by one foot all the way around.

"Gramma," Tucker called. "Roman is here with the ice."

Giant tongs gripped the huge ice block as Roman carried it into the kitchen where he opened the oak icebox. He placed the large block in a compartment near the top of the unit where the cold air would circulate through the insulated box below. "Are you folks still planning to stop ice delivery at the end of the month, Mrs. Moyer?"

"Yes, Roman." Gramma got up from her chair and carried her coffee cup into the kitchen. "We sold a plot of ground for a new family to build their house. We'll buy a refrigerator with the payment when the land deal is settled at the end of the month."

"Is gut, Missus?" The Amish man closed the icebox door and placed the ice tongs on his shoulder. "If you need anything else, just let me know. Remember, I still have my egg, sausage and cheese route. And, my wife makes beautiful quilts, and Grandpa is a busy blacksmith. Send Mr. Moyer over if he needs something forged."

"I will, Roman. Please, keep us on your egg delivery route. I appreciate your hard work." She followed the iceman out to the porch and stood there talking.

After Roman left, Tucker pulled the box of corn flakes down from the cabinet and filled a large bowl. He would be busy that day and needed fuel. Grandpop always said, "If you're going to do a day's work, you can't push a mule uphill without fuel." The milk sloshed a little as he carried it to the side porch and sat on the top step.

The day was glorious. The scent of flowers and grass added a perfume to the air. Tucker shoveled in the crunchy goodness of the flakes and inhaled the morning.

It was Monday, therefore it was laundry day. Each family member had their own task. His eyes popped open as he remembered the baseball gloves. He slipped back into the house, through the kitchen and down to the old stove in the summer house. *Oh no,* he gasped when he saw Grandpop's stack of fire wood on the floor. It wasn't until he grabbed the oven handle and jerked it open that he exhaled. Grandpop hadn't started the fire. The ball gloves were still safe inside. Tucker grabbed them out when he heard his grandfather place his empty cup and saucer in the kitchen sink. With a one handed swoop, Tucker carried the mitts toward the landing, threw them down the basement steps, and then greeted Grandpop at the kitchen door.

With a tone as smooth as honey, Tucker asked. "About ready to start the fire, Grandpop, and get the water going?"

"Ja." Grandpop went down to the summer kitchen, gathered up a few logs and some small sticks for kindling and soon had a fire blazing in the cook stove. He placed a large copper pot on the stove. "Okay, let's go out and get the water."

Tucker's usual job was to help Grandpop fill two buckets at the Ohio-made Myer water pump that stood on a cement pad in the back yard. Each galvanized container was two and a half gallons. They carried them into the summer kitchen where Grandpop filled the huge oval copper boiler waiting on the two-burner cast iron wood stove.

"You're a good help, Tucker."

He smiled and watched for the bubbles to float to the surface of the water. "Thanks Grandpop."

In the winter, when the ground was frozen, the water from the pump was much colder than on a hot day in July. It wouldn't take long to heat it that day. When the water boiled, Grandpop used a long handled ladle to fill the Maytag wringer-washing machine* and the two rinse tubs.

Every washday, Aunt Cora walked down to help with the laundry. Once Gramma put the clothes through the washer, sloshed them through the rinse tubs, and squeezed them through the rollers of the wringer, Aunt Cora placed them in a wicker basket which she carried out into the yard to hang them on the clothes line to dry. It was Tucker's job to help fill the boiler and hang some of the clothes outside.

When they completed the laundry and everything flapped on the line in a light breeze, Tucker came up from the summer kitchen. He checked the clock on the wall above the stove. It was eight o'clock in the morning. Aunt Cora had gone home to do her own family's washing. Gramma didn't slow down, but moved from one job to the next. After all the hub bub on Saturday, with a flying hammock and a special choir practice, Gramma didn't have time to make the week supply of noodles.

"Tucker," Gramma called out as she walked through the living room. "I'm going upstairs to change out of this soapsuds-covered housedress. I may rest a few minutes, too. Then, I'll get busy on the noodles."

"Okay, Gramma." Tucker watched her pull herself up the steps holding onto the banister. He worried about her health and needed another scene to clear his mind. Looking around for something to occupy his need for activity and stimulate his cleaver mind, he grinned.

The Philco radio* they'd listened to last evening stood on four legs with a row of push buttons across the front. It was still early. The *Little Red Barn* program with Bob Sievers would be on WOWO out of Fort Wayne. He pushed the *ON* button. Nancy Lee and the Hilltoppers were singing when the radio warmed up. Tucker flopped down on the floor to listen then jerked up on one elbow. *Great*, he grumbled. There was so much static, the lyrics to the opening theme song crackled. *Stack of new mown hay* sounded more like ... *rack of blue zone day*. Tucker had no idea what a blue zone day was. He knew not to dwell on the words, since the problem was the radio. If the radio weren't fixed, later, when his program started, *The Lone Ranger* could turn out to be *The Grown Stranger.*

First, he studied the outside of the wooden cabinet that held the radio electronics. Along the right side, fresh scratch marks marred the finish. Pieces of popcorn, strewn underneath, were broken into bits. *Tiny?* He knew the dog could have been the sloppy eater who scattered white, popped corn all over the floor, but had no idea what the dog could have done that would cause the weird static.

Without thinking of the possible consequences, Tucker decided, without Uncle Jerry available, "Mr. Fix it" would have to be himself. He'd watched Uncle Jerry fix things any time he had the opportunity to learn. If his uncle could CLEP out of all of his high school classes, certainly Tucker could fix something as simple as a radio.

The thick wood of the cabinet, which was full of tubes, made the Philco very heavy. Tucker placed his hands on both sides of the furniture piece and carefully pulled it out, away from the wall, in order to get behind it. Uncle Jerry always stressed the need for safety when working with electrical things, so Tucker unplugged the unit from the outlet on the wall. With the pen knife he carried in his pocket, he unscrewed the attaching fasteners and removed the back panel.

Removing the body of the radio was the next task. In order to pull the chassis* out of the case he had to remove three knobs from the front of the radio: the on-off switch, the tuning dial, and the volume control. He paused and looked at the mechanism* of the radio from all angles. In order to accomplish the next step he had to take out four bolts from under the radio stand. Studying the radio tubes, he removed them one by one and placed them on the floor in the order in which he took them out.

Over his shoulder and nearly out of his thoughts, Tucker heard the stairs creek but paid little to no attention. He was fixing the radio and couldn't be distracted.

Tucker was so intently working on the radio, he only half-knew Uncle Jacob was standing there watching him. He knew the radio now lay in every piece possible on the living room floor. He guessed his radio overhaul was okay with the family since his uncle said nothing as he worked. When Jacob turned and walked into the kitchen, Tucker was barely aware of that, too.

Tucker had watched Uncle Jerry fix enough electronics in recent months to know he would have to clean the tubes before putting them back in their assigned slots. His handkerchief from his pocket was the ideal dust cloth. After they were clean, to insure a proper seat for the tubes, he pushed down on each one after reinserting them in their socket. Turning the whole chassis on its side, he saw a nest of wires running from the tubes and other components. All looked well. When he went to put the chassis back inside the case, however, he noticed there was a loose screw that held one of the wires to the frame. He tightened the screw, put the chassis back in the case, and bolted it again to the cabinet.

Next, he plugged it in, replaced the knobs, and turned it on. It worked really well, no static at all. Tucker finally looked up and saw his uncle watching him.

There was Uncle Jacob, looking around the corner from the kitchen, smiling. All of the tubes were off the floor and in their proper place. The chassis was also back where it belonged. The Philco stood back in its assigned spot in the living room.

Jacob shook his head in disbelief. Tucker heard him whisper to Gramma, "That boy is sure something. How can he know how to fix something when he's never touched it before? Now if the radio will work, he'll save Jerry the time to fix it."

Tucker smiled quietly when he saw Gramma's expression change from wrinkled worry to relaxed pride out of the corner of his eye. "Will you listen to that?" Gramma whispered back.

Tucker turned up the volume and heard Bob Siever's deep voice flow into the room, creamy and mellow. The airwaves, completely free from static, sounded just as smooth. He stood back and eyed the entire project with pride. *Wonder if I could CLEP out of school and get into Notre Dame University? Maybe not,* he thought as he remembered his last Math quiz.

Chapter 14
Excitement: Good and Bad

Later that day Tucker rolled around on the floor restlessly. The red, gold and blue Oriental rug felt prickly against his cheeks. He pulled up on his elbow and rubbed the rough spot on the carpet. *Never eat in the living room*, Gramma had said more often than Tucker cared to admit. He thought he had cleaned up all the hot cocoa he spilled that evening a few weeks back when he had been alone in the house while Gramma and Grandpop went to a Prayer Meeting at the church. It didn't visibly show but the fibers were stiffer in that spot.

Tucker didn't want to think about yet another time when he had let Gramma down. He'd think about something else. He had read most of the newer magazines he could find from the stack the family kept on the bookcase near the piano. Now, he was itchy to *do something.*

From outside, Tucker heard the rumble of an approaching motorcycle. He could feel it inside his chest. As it came closer, the noise slowed to a mere putter. *It must be slowing.* He pulled the corner of the lace curtain back and saw Freddie prop an Indian chief on its rear stand.

Gramma was making homemade noodles out in the kitchen. Tucker peeked in and saw sheets of rolled thin dough drying on clean tea towels wherever she could find an empty spot to put them. Before she mixed up the next bowlful, she began cutting the slightly dried ones she had rolled out twenty minutes before into noodle-width strips. Tucker knew Gramma would be busy a while longer as she mixed up another batch of eggs, flour, milk and salt. She believed homemade was best since she could add less salt, a wise move given her high blood pressure.

Tucker quietly slipped out the side door with his eye fixed on the magnificent Indian motorcycle Freddie had waiting by the side of the road. "Where'd you get that?" Tucker asked with a muffled yell.

Freddie puffed out his chest and tugged up his pants. "It belongs to my cousin. He said I could ride it while his mom took him to the dentist. He just said to be really careful."

"Can I ride it?" Tucker was nearly drooling as he sized up the blue 1937 Chief.

"Well," Freddie drew out slowly, "if you go slow."

Tucker pouted a little. "Crummy, slow is no fun." He jumped on the bike and settled into the seat. "This is swell."

"Well," Freddie drew out lowly, "I guess."

Tucker looked up and down the street for family who would certainly stop him. With no one around, he pulled away from the house.

"Christopher Columbus, Tucker! Go slow!" Freddie shouted after him, his arms flailing above him.

Houses lined up one after the other in the little community of cousins and close friends behind the white house on the corner. Each home seemed to provide the vibration necessary to create mini-echoes for the whispered roar of the motorcycle. When Tucker turned left onto County Road 13, it was all open riding ahead. No cars were coming into town behind him. No vehicles of any kind were ahead of him, so he saw nothing to stop him. The engine wound out to a high pitched rumbling hum as he picked up speed.

The day was amazing. Blue sky stretched above him with green everywhere else, crops, grass, trees … everywhere. By the time Tucker passed Warren Shaffer's farm, three miles out in the country, the speedometer registered eighty-five miles per hour. He hoped none of the Shaffers were looking out the window or working in the garden. Tucker was even able to maintain the speed when Mr. Shaffer's sheep escaped the apple orchard and came out near the side of the road.

The fast breeze hit Tucker in the face and blew his wavy hair back into a twist. Leaning into the wind he stretched his body out across the bike as he flew farther into farm country. When he neared County Road Thirty, he began to slow, not to a full stop, but enough to make sure he didn't turn the bike over when he turned it around. With the thrill of a Daytona 200 racer, he zipped back toward home.

Turning into the residential cluster of streets he called his neighborhood, he dropped his speed to a whimper. He saw Freddie standing in the middle of the road where Tucker left him, with his hands on his hips.

"You were gone long enough," Freddie grumbled.

"Sorry," Tucker apologized but the ear to ear grin was evidence his ride was worth the time and distance.

Freddie looked at Tucker with a squint in his eye. "Were you careful? Did you drive safe?"

"Oh sure," Tucker brushed him off with his famous smile and a little tease. "I didn't make it to a hundred."

"I hope not," Freddie teased back. His mouth turned upside down as he hopped on the Indian.

When Freddie left, Tucker looked at the house and then thought better of going straight in. Instead, he turned and walked over to the telephone office. He knew Carolyn might be taking a call so he opened the door as quietly as he could.

"My, my, my," Carolyn drew out slowly with a smile and a sigh of relief. "What were you doing? I sent five calls to Gramma in the last few minutes."

Tucker's smile faded. Suddenly, he realized that everyone he passed along the route reported his antics to Gramma again. "I was riding Freddie Cooper's cousin's motorbike."

"Riding? Or, flying?" Carolyn studied Tucker's expression.

"All Gramma asked was that I didn't worry Grandpop." Looking down, his voice dropped to a whisper. "I forgot about her blood pressure."

"Tucker, you're a great boy." Carolyn reassured him. "Like Rev. Dailey says, you're the Dunlap Kid."

"I might have heard that." Tucker hung his head. "I guess that's better than being called Billy the Kid," Tucker decided.

"If Momma were here," Carolyn checked for any light on the switch board before she went on, "would you be riding a motorcycle on country roads at break-neck speeds?"

A sheepish grin spread across his face as he drew out slowly, "Yeah. What's wrong with riding a motorcycle?"

"Well," Carolyn thought for a second, "did you ever worry that you might get caught?"

The image of Shaffer's wooly sheep popped into his mind. He had to admit, to himself if not to Carolyn, he had wondered if anyone in the family was home. "Maybe, just a minute." He shifted uneasily from one foot to the other. "You said five people called Gramma?"

"Yep," she assured him as she drew the corner of her mouth back.

"But, you don't know who was calling…" he stopped and pointed his finger at his sister. "You were listening."

Carolyn gave away her surprise when her eyes popped open. "I most certainly was not."

Tucker drug the tip his shoe into the floor. "Maybe it was the dentist's office, reminding her about an appointment."

"She doesn't have a dentist appointment coming up."

"Oh, okay. I really didn't think about her blood pressure. Sometimes I lay awake at night when I hear her cough and wonder if she's okay."

"Well, hallelujah, Tucker. I'm glad you're thinking about her health. She isn't young you know. That's why I help her watch out for you."

Tucker's eyes twinkled with mischief. "I know. Gramma can't run fast enough to catch me."

Carolyn's eyes narrowed. "You must remember, Tucker, that little lady raised five children, Monday through Friday of every week, all by herself. Grandpa was at work on the railroad, anywhere between Chicago and Toledo, Ohio. And, she can take care of you, too. You're a good kid. Don't you think she deserves a few calm days?"

"Sure, but I…"

"That's the problem, Tucker. I." Carolyn checked the switchboard again. "I think maybe it's your stubbornness again."

"You know about my stubborn side?" Tucker couldn't believe that his sister knew he had two sides.

She threw her head back and laughed. "Tucker, the whole neighborhood knows you're stubborn, in a very good-natured way of course. You want to do things your way. You don't argue about it. You just do it, or don't do it."

Tucker smiled a little when he remembered his conversation with his grandmother. "Gramma sort of said the same thing."

Carolyn jumped as another call came in. She turned and got back to her job at the switchboard. "Yes, what number please?" With her hand over the mouth piece, she mouthed, "I'll be home for supper."

Tucker walked out of the little telephone switch station and across Moyer Avenue. He moseyed* much slower than his usual run, dragging one foot more than the previous. *Wonder how many people called Gramma?*

He stepped in through the door slowly, trying to get the *temperature* inside before he made his presence known. No one in the house raised their voice; no one even glanced in Tucker's direction. He wondered if anyone missed him.

"Several people called to say you were riding somebody's motorcycle." Gramma didn't even look up from her noodle making. "Whose bike was it?"

"A cousin of Freddie Cooper's," Tucker sensed it was safe to go as far into the kitchen as the cookie jar. He removed two large oatmeal raisin baked treats from Gramma's stash.

"Don't spoil your meal, now. I'll finish with these noodles in a few minutes. We'll have a nice roast." She continued to cut the last of the noodles into their proper width and lay them out on the flour dusted tea towels to dry.

"I'm starved. I don't think I could spoil any meal."

"Ja, Tuck, some day. Don't worry about it today." Gramma brushed flour from her apron and rubbed her aching fingers together. "Worry isn't good for anyone, Tucker."

Tucker was thankful no one at home yelled, no one scolded. He did, however, recognize the recent theme, don't cause Gramma to worry. On the one hand everyone in the neighborhood kept their eye on Tucker and passed the information on to his grandmother, intending to help her keep track of him. Sometimes it felt like he was the subject of a police investigation, with everyone in the neighborhood acting as a C.I., a Confidential Informant. However, he wasn't a criminal. Still, he had learned a quiet lesson. Tell Gramma the truth but not to the point of worrying her.

Chapter 15
A Good Idea

"Where do ya think you're going?" Carolyn asked Tucker later as he headed for the side door. With a long handled cooking fork in her hand, Carolyn lifted the last small bite of roast from Gramma's cast iron roaster and offered the piece to Tucker. "This is an extra piece so you have the energy to dry the dishes."

The delicious smell of browned chuck roast cooked with potatoes and carrots still hung in the air. Normally, the last meal of the day on a hot July evening would have been lighter. This time, Gramma had even cooked some of her freshly made noodles in the beef broth. When Delbert Mays brought a fine little piece of meat suitable for roasting by the house to thank Grandpop for the use of a special tool for hanging a door, there was only one answer to Tucker's usual question, "What's for dinner?"

Tucker was thrilled when Delbert provided the dinner fixings, too. Mays brought two jars with the roast; one was his Molly's delicious canned small carrots and the other, a large quart jar of round white potatoes.

The root cellar* in the back yard was empty by now. Tucker had helped Grandpop dig the long, wide hole, line it with gunny sacks, then pile in layer after layer of the fall garden harvest, separated by more sacks and straw. Grandpop made the entire root cellar safe by surrounding the whole thing with a short, three foot high temporary fence to mark the spot. Also, Gramma still had a few jars of canned fruit and vegetables in the basement. Those had to last until canning season came around again, or until the cherry and apple trees were once again heavy with fruit. Luckily, that would be soon.

Tucker stole a quick glance at Gramma before he talked back to his oldest sister. "Just 'cause you're older than me doesn't mean you're my boss."

Betsy joined in and swatted Tucker with the tea towel she hung on her shoulder. "Everyone in this house is older than you, brother." She laughed as she added hot water to the pan from Gramma's old dented tea kettle.

"All right, you three," Gramma said as she flapped the bottom of her flowered apron at Tucker. "Betsy, I can't see you have much to laugh about. Haven't I told you to wear a cotton skirt? Pants aren't proper for a girl."

"But Gramma…" Betsy protested. "How can I play baseball with a skirt on?"

"Never mind baseball," Gramma cautioned. "Grandpa has need of Tucker's help," she added, dismissing the boy. "Now, run along young man. Grandpa is already over at the church."

Tucker turned up his nose at his sisters while he pushed on the screen door. "If one of you can carry five gallon buckets of cinders out of the basement, I'll dry the dishes and you go over and help Grandpop." Tucker smiled an impish smile.

Since Grandpop's doctor refused to let him carry the heavy buckets, the job fell to Tucker's growing muscles. Grandpop's doctor was a member of the church, and Joseph could lose his job as church janitor if he didn't follow medical orders.

"I could do it," Betsy called after Tucker, bragging. "You know I wouldn't want to show you up though, Tucker."

That warm July evening Grandpa had planned to clean out the bottom section of the huge church furnace. Tucker remembered that last snow in March, deep and heavy to the shovel, when he graduated to a one-handed lift of one of the buckets full of remnants of burned coal. His grandfather paid him a quarter to carry out twelve gigantic pails, one at a time. That evening in July, however, *The Lone Ranger* radio program was going to start in half an hour. Tucker had already fixed the radio and warmed his spot on the carpet to stretch out and listen.

Down in the basement of the church, the smell of dry coal dust lingered in the air. His grandfather had already filled two five gallon buckets when Tucker bounced down the concrete steps. I'm here Grandpop," he said.

"Ja," Tucker. "Das ist gut*." Grandpop pointed to both of the full buckets and stood back. "Those two are ready. Grab one, Tucker."

"Gramma said I should ask you about something I could make for Uncle Jacob's birthday." Tucker looked down at the buckets and sighed. Twelve buckets equaled twelve trips up the steps. *The Lone Ranger* could already be on by the time he'd finished the last one.

"She did say something about that gift," Grandpop stuck the square-scoop coal shovel into the ash pile again. "We'll go out to the workshop after we're done here and have a look around."

Tucker closed his eyes and gulped. "Sure Grandpop," he said. But, his inner thoughts were, *Oh no. I trapped myself. I'll miss my radio program.* Tucker eyed the row of buckets already filled. Grandpop had just dumped cinders into the fourth bucket. A cloud of ash dust caused Tucker to cough. He wiped his nose on his sleeve and studied the cluster of containers for a minute.

Tucker's own wet nose reminded him of Gary Straum's dog out at Straum's Dairy Farm. The last time he rode with Uncle Jacob out to the dairy, the Straum's German shepherd, Oscar, was so happy to see him again the dog wiped his runny nose on Tucker's blue jeans. Oscar's breath smelled like dog, but Tucker didn't care. The shepherd reminded him of the best dog in the world, Joe. Tucker remembered another piece of helpful information from that last time he'd gone out to the dairy for the family's weekly supply of milk. While there, he watched Gary grab two full, ten gallon milk cans in each hand and swing them from side to side. The momentum* helped Gary build up the rhythm to carry the cans, full of eighty-five pounds of whole milk, all the way out to the road for pick up.

Tucker looked at the growing cluster of filled buckets, took a deep breath and steadied himself. Wrapping his hands around two bucket handles, he picked them up on an upswing. Swaying them back and forth, he danced them up the steps, out the door, and into the parking lot behind the church.

That was easy, he bragged to himself. When he got back downstairs, he eyed the remaining ten buckets and decided, this time, he'd grab two handles in each hand. Doing the swinging dance step again, to the beat of *Down in my Heart,* he boogied* the buckets up and out of the basement. Clustering the large cans outside the back door, he turned and shouted, "The lone ranger rides again!" With a running jump, Tucker skipped down a few steps and landed on the concrete floor in front of his grandfather.

"Seven more, Tucker," Grandpa said as he smiled. "You're doin' gut."

"Thanks, Grandpop." Tucker didn't often get praise for doing his work. Both of his grandparents expected him to always do his best. Gathering up four more handles, he repeated the upstairs race he was running with the clock, and then returned for the last three. "That's it, Grandpop. I'm going back to the house now," Tucker started up the stairs, hoping his grandfather wouldn't think of the other chore.

"Hold on there, Tucker," Grandpa called after him. "Two more things: first, we have to spread these ashes. Then, we'll go over to the shop to see what supplies might be there for Jacob's present." Grandpop walked over to one of the many puddle holes in the muddy area to the back of the parking lot behind the church and pointed to the first bucket. "Right here Tucker."

Tucker studied the size of the pothole. "Looks like a three bucket fill."

"Ja. The rain the other day increased the size of all of the holes." Grandpop poised his shovel at the side of the puddle while Tucker tipped up one bucket after the other. He dumped and Grandpop spread the coal cinders around. After he filled the last pothole, his grandfather used the shovel handle to point in the direction of his workshop.

Together, they walked across the church parking lot, crossed the street, and into the Moyer side yard. Grandpa built the workshop on the far edge of the yard. He had used lumber given to him or pieces neighbors dropped off in exchange for the use of a tool. The wooden structure was sound with a silver patina after heavy snows and years of rain pelted the building. Tucker removed the padlock that dangled from the latch Grandpa created from a solid oak slide bolt. Grandpop always left the workshop unlocked during the day. No one would disturb his tools. In fact, Grandpa loaned them out freely. He had only one requirement … "ya daresn't loss it*."

"I'll get the lights." Grandpop reached around inside the door and flipped the switch.

Tucker stepped into the most magical room he knew. It smelled like the hard forged metal of hammer heads, mixed with the aroma of leather and sawdust. There were saws and screw drivers of all kinds.

Joseph would take discarded, broken tools home from work on the weekend, repair them, and hang them on his workshop wall. In addition to his usual duties, anytime a railway bridge or trestle was involved in an accident on the line between Elkhart and Chicago, the company called him in. Covering the walls of his workshop were tools most of his friends couldn't even name.

Grandpa looked around the shop. "What do ya think?"

"Well …." Tucker studied the room but couldn't focus. His mind, fixed on his favorite radio program, bounced from workbench, to the wood stored above the high ceiling beams. "I don't know. Have you got any ideas, Grandpop?"

"Well now, Tucker. This is your gift. If I were you, I'd think about the things Uncle Jacob likes to do."

Tucker's eyes brightened. Maybe he did have an idea. "Yep, I can think of something."

"Now what would that be?" Grandpop asked, placing his hand on Tuck's shoulder.

"I want to keep that a secret."

Grandpop raked his fingers through his thinning gray hair. "Now, Tucker, we can't put any money to it, but I might be able to call in some return favors for small supplies." He smiled and flipped off the lights. "You run along, but tomorrow, you'd better get busy on your project. Oh, instead of a quarter, here's fifty cents for all the hauling you did this evening. You earned it with those extra buckets in both hands. You're getting stronger every day."

"Thanks, Grandpop," Tucker called back as he stuffed the fifty cent piece deep into his jeans pocket. He darted across the yard, in through the summer kitchen door and up the few steps into the kitchen. He quickly slowed to a causal walk as he entered the living room. Gramma was sitting in the platform rocker with her mending in her lap.

Yeah! He yelled inside, giving an internal shout of a job completed. Tucker slid into the living room and onto the rug in front of the Philco. Betsy slouched on the couch with her feet on a *McCall's* magazine she had placed on the coffee table to protect the marble finish.

As the program began, Tucker put his hands under his head, smiled with satisfaction and closed his eyes. As the deep throated announcer began, Tucker mouthed the words along with the voice from the radio.

"In the early days of the western United States, a masked man and an Indian rode the plains, searching for truth and justice. Return with us now to those thrilling days of yesteryear, when, from out of the past, come the thundering hoof-beats of the great horse Silver. The Lone Ranger rides again!"

Chapter 16
The Shiny Bike

The early morning mid-summer sky could not have been bluer than if God had spilled His best can of sweet-azure paint across the wide expanse of heaven. It was 6:30AM. Tucker had already been up for half an hour. He sat on the small side porch sharing his cornflakes with Tiny. Gramma often cautioned the family to not eat more than their share of any of the food. Corn flakes were different. Tucker usually ate half a box and sometimes the entire thing every day.

Gramma was in the kitchen using her sprinkling bottle with the aluminum multi-holed top to dampen her laundry before ironing. Every piece of clothing she had washed the day before was lightly sprinkled with water, rolled up and put in the laundry basket. Later that day, she would iron each one of them dry, removing all the wrinkles.

Grandpop was up at his usual time, four AM, put on a pot of coffee and dropped some of Gramma's thick sweet bread into the side drop-down toaster*. The toasty aroma still filled the kitchen. By the time Tucker came out of the house, Grandpop was in the garden gathering the last of the strawberries for Gramma's huge strawberry shortcake she said she'd make for supper.

"Here, Tiny." Tucker offered the little dog the last three pieces of the toasted flakes of corn. The boy took his blue handkerchief out of his pocket and wiped Tiny's hairy chin. "When you go back inside, you better not get even a drop of milk on Gramma's rug."

Freddie Cooper came walking past just as Grandpop brought the berries up out of the garden. "Freddie," Joseph acknowledged. "Ya want some coffee?"

Tucker's friend looked at him with a quizzical expression. "No Sir, thank you. I don't drink coffee."

Grandpop shook the berry basket a little, releasing sweetness into the air. Tucker couldn't get enough of the strawberry perfume. "Tucker doesn't drink coffee either," his grandfather admitted. "Sometimes during the cold months, he breaks some bread up in a bowl or large cup, pours coffee over the top and sprinkles a teaspoon or two of sugar over the top."

"Never had that before," Freddie said softly, while the corners of his mouth turned down.

Tucker jumped into the conversation before Grandpop could offer his friend a sampling of *coffee soup*. "You're up early Freddie. Ya know it's still summer vacation."

"I know. Pa wanted me to come over to ask your grandpa if he could borrow his number five hand plane. Dad's working second shift now. This morning, he wants to smooth out the edges of a new kitchen counter he's building for Ma before he goes to work after lunch."

Grandpop asked, "Your pa's on second shift?" He placed the basket of strawberries on the porch and slowly straightened his back, bent from exposure to the damp morning air. "The factory must still be switching back from war time production."

"Yeah, I guess." Freddie stuffed his hands in his pockets. "The factory will be cutting back soon since the war's over. Dad wants to get in as much over-time hours as possible. He'll go back to his old schedule, working on the day shift, in two weeks. The factory will be making switches for radios soon."

"Ja." Grandpop turned toward the back yard again. "I'll fetch the hand plane."

"Thanks," Freddie relaxed a little. "My dad will be mad if I don't get home quick. Does your pa get mad at you, too?"

"My pa?" Tucker's shoulders sagged a little. "No. Sometimes I think that would be nice." Tucker's eyes followed a 1939 green Hudson as it pulled slowly off the highway and stopped at the sidewalk. A man got out. He wore frayed brown pants and a white shirt with rolled up sleeves. Half tied, his necktie hung loosely around his neck with the top of his shirt unbuttoned.

Freddie looked from the man to Tucker. "That guy looks familiar. Does he go to our church?"

Tucker put his hand to his mouth and mumbled hoarsely. "No. I don't know if he's ever been in a church."

In the dim corner of his mind, Tucker did remember a time when his father showed up at the church after a Sunday evening service. Family stories of what happened reminded Tucker that he was about two years old at the time. That day so long ago, he could feel his heart beat as Gramma held him tightly in her arms. Tucker's own sense of odor detection reminded him that his father smelled funny during that struggle, a little like a bottle of Gramma's real vanilla that had gone bad. Tucker could still feel Sean grabbing at his hands and legs, trying to pull him out of Gramma's arms and drag him away. He remembered crying. To protect him, several men of the church forced Sean to leave. He had no right to take Tucker anywhere. The judge had already made a ruling. Tucker and his sisters and brother now belonged to Gramma and Grandpop Moyer, with Uncle Jacob appointed as their legal guardian. Yes, Tucker knew his dad had been in the church … at least once.

"Who is he?" Freddie asked again.

Before Tucker could answer, Grandpop came back with the Stanley woodworking tool.

"Morning, Sean," Grandpop greeted, but his enthusiasm seemed measured.

"Hi, Dad," Tucker walked slowly over to the car.

"Dad?" Freddie gasped as Joseph handed him the rosewood handled plane.

"Now, ya daresn't loss it," he repeated his well-known phrase.

"I'll be very careful with it. Dad said to tell you, he'll drop it off on his way to work." Freddie took the plane and looked over at Tucker with a puzzled look. "See ya, Tucker."

"See ya," Tucker called after him, and then walked over to his dad slowly, shuffling a pebble back and forth along the sidewalk.

Grandpop touched the bill of his striped railroad cap and picked up the strawberries. "I'll go in the house and get a little more coffee." That left Tucker some time with his father. "We'll go out to the workshop again soon."

"Tucker," Sean put his hand on Tuck's shoulder. "It was good to see you the other day in the store. I brought something for you." He opened the trunk lid. There, neatly packed and braced was a new, deep maroon Schwinn auto-cycle deluxe bicycle with white stripes. "It's yours, Tucker," Sean said with pride. "The Garland Department Store had two new 1941 bicycles back in storage. When our country became involved in the war, Schwinn converted most all of their factories in the U.S. to war production. New bicycles will come out sometime soon but this one is new, too. It's new old stock."

"Jeepers, Dad, thanks." Tucker reached in the trunk and started to pull it out. He hesitated, "Can I?"

"It's yours," his dad said and smiled. "Someone told me you needed a bike without a motor. Go ahead and take it out of the trunk. I have to get to work."

"Keen," Tucker squealed. "It has twin headlights, front breaks, built-in speedometer, and a neat tank and chain guard."

"What ya got there?" Tim came out and stood on the porch with his arms folded.

"A super bike," Tucker answered without looking away from the shiny frame. When the classy Schwinn bike finally rested safely on the ground, Tucker checked Tim's expression. Since he was the oldest of the McBride four, he acted like he was Tucker's boss. Looking past Tim, his feet planted wide and determined, he saw Grandpop through the kitchen window sipping his coffee.

Tiny pranced over and sniffed around the bike wheels. Regardless of how long they'd been stored, the tires still smelled like new rubber. Tucker wondered why the store hadn't taken the tires off the bike when there was a War-effort rubber drive, collecting all things made out of the black substance.

Tim stepped down off the porch and slowly walked out to the Hudson. Would he acknowledge the McBride kids' dad or snap at him. "Sean," Timothy nodded. Rarely did he ever call him Dad or Pop. He kept the man at a distance. On that day, at least he was polite.

Relieved that Tim didn't argue with Sean or jealously say something hurtful about their dad or the bicycle, Tucker jabbed the kickstand with his foot and hoped on. When he heard the brake snap into place, he was ready to go. "Thanks, Dad," Tucker shouted back as he rode down the street. Tiny ran and jumped, following beside him, while his ears flapped in the morning air.

Tucker's insides bubbled with joy, but it rattled his heart as well. He didn't know how he was supposed to feel about his father. Was he supposed to dislike him, or … was it all right to love him … just a little?

"Mighty nice bike," Grandpop called to Tucker as he came out onto the porch again. He turned to Sean and waved as McBride got back in his car. "Thanks. I know Tucker is happy."

Sean McBride waved at Tucker, started his car and pulled away. He paused at the highway, then pulled his car in the direction of Goshen.

Tucker brought the bike back to the sidewalk and jumped off. "Grandpop, is it okay if I like him a little?"

"You can never have too many people who love you and who you love in return. Don't let anyone tell you who to love or who not." He put his hand on Tucker's shoulder, "A boy has a right to love his father."

Tucker climbed back on his new bike and peddled down the street. The sweet morning breeze blew through his hair as he released his hands from the handle bars, closed his eyes, and sailed past Freddie's house no-handed. Mr. Cooper was just walking in the house with Grandpop's plane in his hand. Tucker smiled but his heart didn't.

Chapter 17
The Best Wood for the Best Idea

Tucker biked on around the corner onto Franklin Street. Christy was just coming out of her house and grabbed her bike from where she had left it beside the garage. "Hey, Christy, don't ya know you shouldn't leave your bike outside at night?"

"Good honk, Tucker," Christy gasped, "if I had a new bike like yours I'd lock it up at night, too. Where'd you get it?"

"My … dad dropped it off just a little while ago."

"Your dad? You just saw him in Goshen and now he came by the house? Great!"

Tucker angled his front tire back onto the pavement. "I'm testing this out."

"Okay, I'll ride along," Christy offered. Behind her, Rosie waddled along at a pace rarely seen in swine.

"Suit yourself." Tucker pulled away from Christy's driveway with her following. He looked back and watched Rosie's little short legs trying to keep up with the wheels of the two bicycles. Tuck thought of Joe's long sleek gait and smiled.

Tucker remembered when Joe ran; all four feet were off the ground at the same time for a split second. He ran so fast, his hind feet would reach beyond the print left by the front feet. *What a dog!*

Tucker couldn't think about Joe any more. As he and Christy peddled back toward the Moyer home, Tucker's speed increased. Running away, if only for a few blocks, was what might free him from the image of his big, gentle, heroic dog who saved many G.I.s' lives in the war … and then couldn't come home.

"Hey, Tucker, what ya doing?" Christy called after him. "Are we racing now?"

Tucker said no more, but kept on pedaling. As they rounded the corner onto Moyer Avenue, he looked up from his intense pace and saw Tim step out onto the porch again. He knew if he pushed too hard racing back to the house, his brother would say something about not being responsible. Something like, "You'll wreck that fancy new bike."

Christy's expression also changed when she saw Tim standing there with his hands on his hips. Tucker's brother had a way of teasing her, making Christy feel uncomfortable. Mostly, he liked to call her by her full name, Christmas Tree.

"Well, good morning, Miss Tree," Tim said with a grin. "We have Christmas in July right here in our yard. Have you baked any cookies today?"

"Knock it off, Timothy" Tucker hissed.

"Knock it off?" Tim bellowed. "Where'd you suddenly get your backbone?"

"Never mind." Tucker hopped off his bike and walked it into the yard. "Christy, come on back to Grandpop's workshop." He looked down at the pig. "Rosie, you can come, too."

"Hey, you guys," Freddie called out as he walked onto the narrow sidewalk. "What's up?" Freddie took another bite of the largest doughnut twist Tucker had ever seen.

Tucker knew Mrs. Cooper was a great baker because he always made sure he got a piece of her pie or cake at church carry-in dinners before it was all gone. Now he was face to face with another of her specialties, yeast doughnuts in a variety of sizes and shapes.

"We're going to Grandpop's workshop for a creative summit." Tucker turned to make sure Rosie was behind them. Many people in the area didn't like the idea of a pig roaming around the neighborhood. He wanted to make sure the pork chop was close to the other summit members.

Tim stepped down onto the sidewalk. "When are you going to make bacon out of that pig, Christmas Tree?"

"That's diabolical*, Timothy Archibald McBride." Christy screamed over her shoulder. She didn't even look back.

Tim's jaw tightened. "How'd you know my middle name?"

She turned and sassed back in a volume loud enough for anyone around to hear. "Archibald Baldy McBride."

He looked around for anyone who may have heard, then stomped back into the house.

Tucker and his two allies continued across the yard to Grandpop's workshop. As he opened the squeaky rustic door, he smiled at the familiar sounds and old-world smells. Inside the workshop, the three looked from high to low. Even Rosie checked out the exotic tools that hung on the walls and clustered in wooden trunks.

"Snazzy," Christy whispered on exhale. "I don't even know what these things are called."

"Tools," Freddie offered as he scanned the room. "Just … tools."

Christy searched each gadget and contraption in the workshop. "Why are we in here?"

"We begin here." Tucker reached for the piece of thick birds-eye maple wood Grandpop had laid out for him last evening. He placed it on Grandpop's workbench where the three stared at it for what seemed to Tucker, the longest time.

"What is it?" Christy asked.

"Birds-eye maple."

She studied it slowly. "Yes … but I mean, besides being a pretty board."

Tucker ran his fingers over the wood with all its squiggles and figures. "That's what I want you guys to help me decide."

Freddie studied the wood with what appeared to be tiny swirling eyes. "Decide what?"

Tucker sighed deeply. "Uncle Jacob's birthday is on the fourth of July. I want to make him a great present but that's two days from now. What do I make out of this board?"

The piece of lumber was long and wide. To Tucker, it didn't look like anything in particular. Somehow, a present was going to have to leap out of the wood grain and introduce itself to Tucker, like a genie out of a bottle, if he was going to make a gift in such a short length of time. "Any ideas?"

Freddie said nothing for a moment. Then his eyes brightened. "What does he like to do? Does he have any hobbies?"

"He works, reads, and gardens," Tucker skimmed off the top of his uncle's world.

"Tucker," Christy put her hands on her hips. "What else?"

He thought for a minute and smiled as quiet evenings at home filled his mind. "On Sunday evenings, Gramma reads her Bible, Grandpop works a couple of crossword puzzles, and Uncle Jacob plays his violin."

"Of course, that would be his hobby, Tucker." Then, Christy added, "His music sounded really nice." Christy touched the wood and smiled. "Put it down on the floor so I can see how big it is."

"The floor?" Tucker protested.

"Sure." She stepped out of the way to make room for the plank.

The wood thudded as Tucker lowered it to the floor. Wood dust created a small cloud that hung over the room and made him cough again.

The piece of wood stretched across the open space and nearly tucked itself up under the workbench. Christy started at one end and began stepping it off. "My feet are small, but if I walk with a causal stride I can get a pretty good idea of how long it is." She strolled from one end of the maple to the other. "Looks like about six feet."

"And … about a third as wide," Tucker concluded. "Maybe two feet wide."

Freddie scratched his head and wrinkled his brow. "What ya going to make out of it? I can't see anything in that hunk of wood but a barrel of toothpicks."

Rosie made soft grunting noises, toddled onto the wood, stretched out all four legs and made oinking sounds. "That means she's content," Christy laughed. "You may not get her to move. She's in her cradle, even if it's flat and hard as a board."

Tucker jumped in the air. The pig startled as Tucker shouted. "Cradle?" he squealed, almost as loud as Rosie. "That's it."

"It is?" Freddie whipped around, dropping the last bite of his doughnut on the dusty floor.

"Freddie," Tucker gasped, hoping the piece didn't touch the board. "That could make a greasy spot on the wood."

"It's okay," Freddie protested as he ran his sticky finger through his hair. "I know it didn't touch your birthday board. It hit the ground." Freddie picked up the bite, brushed it off on his shirt and popped it into his mouth.

"Yuck," Christy gagged. "You'll eat anything won't you?"

"If my mom made it … yep."

Tucker wondered what his own mother's baked goods had tasted like. Gramma made a pie for every day of the week … apple was his favorite. But … he still wondered. However, he didn't wonder any more about what he'd make for Uncle Jacob. He knew.

Chapter 18
Working Men Work

Unsettled by his dad's visit, Tucker found it hard to concentrate on the project. Still, he was determined to make Uncle Jacob's present and make it right.

Wonder what I'll need besides the wood. It didn't matter; Gramma and Grandpop were on a very tight budget. If he was going to put any extra money into it beyond the wood, Tucker knew he'd have to make money on his own. He needed a job.

If it were a little later in the summer, he could dig potatoes for several of the big truck farmers in the area. While he'd never done it before, friends had talked about it. Then there was last week when he had helped other kids in the area detassel a field of corn. It was a muddy, sweaty job but he needed to save back some money for basketball shoes for next winter's season. Tucker had made the junior high basketball team. He couldn't spend that money. Saving the earnings he already had was the only way he could get the shoes for sure.

What am I going to do? Tucker sat in the crook of one of the cherry trees in the side yard orchard. Fruit trees aren't very tall so Tucker figured he was safe with Gramma.

I could ask Dad. Tucker's body shuddered. He had never asked his father for anything. He was afraid if he did ask him for money, his dad would say no. And, if he started asking for help now, he didn't know if he could stop. So, that was out.

Across the street, beside Winkler's grocery store, Butch Randolf's Sinclair filling station and attached two bay repair garage was one of Tucker's favorite places. The lights on the red, visible gas pumps with Sinclair Gas globes on the top announced when they were open.

"That's it." Tucker made one grand leap out of the tree and hit the ground running. He started across the street dodging a car that whipped around in front of the station.

Butch was in the station's office; Tucker could see him through the large window. Everyone around the neighborhood knew Butch. He was a quiet guy with a good sense of humor.

"Hey, Butch," Tucker bounded through the door with new found enthusiasm. "Do you have any work for me to do?"

"Work? Sure … sure always," Butch said as he tilted his head and seemed to think through his day. "A fellow brought in a tractor tire and needed it fixed right away. Said he had a whole day's work waitin' for him. I told him I already had fifteen other tires ahead of him."

Tucker's eyes popped. "I'll fix it for you."

Butch looked at him with a squint in his eye. "Okay. Go ahead."

Tucker darted through the door between the station office and the garage. Along the back wall of the building, a rack of tires leaned one on the other. *Wow!* Tucker's eyes popped. Butch would pay him by the tire. Each one was a little more money.

Tucker looked at the large tractor tire, the last one on the rack. He had only seen Butch patch an inner tube of a tire a few times but he was sure he remembered what the boss had done.

"Oh, hi Tucker." Christy walked her bicycle to the end of the garage bay on the right. From there she could see Tucker studying the tractor tire. "Are you working here?"

"Yep." He patted the tire with busy hands.

Christy twisted the handle bars back and forth. "Mr. Randolf, I need some air in my front tire."

A small crooked smile crept across Butch's lips. "Sure. Tucker will you please pump it for her? Ever since I reopened after I got back from the war, I've been running as fast as I can to catch up to the work that was waiting for me."

"Happy to," the boy puffed out proudly, a real worker in a respected place of business. "The air pump is over there." Tucker pointed Christy to the right of the building.

Christy walked her bike in lock-step with Tucker. The red pump with a dial above and a long hose wrapped in a circle around a bracket in the middle was at the side of the station, up against the wall.

"Arf, arf," Tiny yipped as she started to dart across the street.

"No!" Christy yelled.

A driver in a 1939 Ford, two door business coupe screeched to a halt within inches of the fuzz on Tiny's ears. The little dog turned, barked and bounced up and down at the front fender of the car.

"Tiny," Tucker ordered and pointed toward the house. "Get home. Go on," he waved his index finger to his house across the street. "Go!"

Tiny looked at Tucker and Christy, then skipped back across the street and joined Rosie waiting by the berm of the road on the Moyer side. Once there, Tiny lay down in the grass at the end of the front sidewalk and folded her paws over, one on top of the other. She placed her chin on her paws and sighed deeply.

"Joe used to take care of that little family member." Tucker smiled as he thought about the two dogs.

Christy looked over at the forlorn expression on the silky. "Whatcha mean?"

Tucker stuffed his hands in his pockets. "One day Roman Swartz pulled up to the side of the house. He had a tray of eggs, sausage, cheese, bread and donuts. Tiny yipped and barked and jumped at Mr. Swartz's feet. Roman dodged the yapper but still nearly tripped. Gramma told Tiny to get out of the way, but Tiny wouldn't obey. So, Joe picked her up by the nap of the neck and flipped her over his shoulder across the hedge, back into the grass. Tiny landed on her feet like a cat. Yipping and whining all the way to the side porch, she sat there all morning, nursing her humiliation."

Tears gathered in the corners of Christy's eyes. "Joe was a good dog."

"Yep," was all Tucker could get out. Any more words would have choked in his throat.

"Okay then," Christy stated with determination. "How about the air in my tire? Don't want to make you lose work time."

Tucker released the coiled hose from the stand and attached the air chuck*, the special tire clamp, to the tire's valve. He watched the gauge carefully to make sure the tire wasn't over-inflated. "Done," Tucker announced and released the handle.

Christy nudged Tucker on the arm as Old Noah, the scraggly man who lived down near the low end of the creek, pulled up in his 1925 Maxwell Touring car. "Look at that," she stifled* a giggle. Covering her mouth, she tried not to insult the old man.

Noah got out of the car and walked over to the boy, his back bent over so far, with every step, he stared at the ground. "Tucker," he turned his head to the side as he tried to look up at Tuck. "Glad I saw you here." He reached into his pocket and pulled out a small brown leather coin purse with a squeeze-it closure. "I owe you fifty cents for weeding my garden last week. Can't work with my buggered up arm." He handed the money to Tucker and put his coin catcher away.

"How'd you hurt it?" Christy asked.

"I was in the barn, paintin' the car, and stumbled over a pitch fork." He turned and beamed at his car. "Do ya like the color?"

"Well…" Christy drew out as she looked at the decades old automobile, from the proudly seated head lights to the back bumper. She pretended to cough, which covered the giggles that appeared to be more than she could control. "Were the feathers added for accent?"

"Well, not added by me." Noah scratched his head and shrugged, like it made no matter anyway. "I'd just finished painting the blue, when I tripped over the pitch fork. Then, the fork hit the stall where some of the chickens were pecking around. The hens clucked and fluttered and flew over the stall railings. Feathers flew everywhere. Since I hurt my arm when I fell, I couldn't shoo them off fast enough, and since I couldn't scatter them back into the barn yard, their feathers fluttered down and landed on the Maxwell's new paint while it was still wet." He paused and beamed proudly at his masterpiece. "But, do you like the color?"

Christy's mouth hung open but Tucker jumped into the silence and covered for her. "That's a mighty pretty blue, Noah," he reached over and patted him on the shoulder.

Noah straightened up as much as his bent back would permit. "Gotta run." He waved his hand in the air as he started for his classic car. "And, you gotta get back to work."

"Thanks, Noah," Tucker called after him.

Tucker and Christy watched as Noah got into his car and pulled back onto the highway. As soon as his front tire hit the pavement, like Mt Vesuvius, the two burst into laughter, held their breath and rocked back and forth.

Christy covered her mouth and staggered to her bicycle. "What a hoot! Thanks Tucker, for the air and the laugh. Now … get back to work." They both laughed. Christy got on her bike, peddled away, while adding, "Gotta run."

Tucker watched her as she crossed the highway and disappeared onto the side street of the neighborhood. He was excited to turn his attention to the tires Butch had for him to fix. Hard work would produce money, his money.

He took down the large tractor tire. First, Tucker removed the valve stem, and then used the tire bead breaker to pull the tire from the rim. He put some air in the tube and tested it in water for leaks. Wherever there were bubbles, there were leaks. When he found the hissing puncture point, he dried the tube and took it over to the work bench. There, he put the tire on Butch's anvil, roughing up the hole in the tube with a wire brush to make the rubber patch stick. Then he put the tube back in the tire, making sure there were no wrinkles in it. When he added more air, the tire was re-inflated.

Tucker turned down the blaring radio on a shelf just to the side of the door that connected the office with the garage. "It's done," he said as he walked back over to where Butch was changing oil in Pastor Daily's sedan.

Butch looked at the large tire, bounced it on the floor, and patted Tucker on the back. "It looks good. You want to do any of the others back there?"

Tucker nearly jumped up and down. "I'll do them all!"

"Well, do as many as you can." Butch turned the radio up and leaned over the Ford again.

The row of tires didn't look impossible to Tucker. Instead, it looked like a challenge … and Tucker loved a challenge. He took down the first tire, went through the patching process and grinned. "One down … fourteen to go," he ticked off aloud.

He knew he could finish every one of them. Somehow, it was easy for him to work from one tire to another without a break or a snack.

"How you doin'?" Butch asked as he wiped his oily hands on a red shop rag. "I just put sparkplugs in Principal Jarvis's car. I noticed you've been keeping up with me."

"I finished the last one," Tucker announced with his chest also inflated.

"Wow. You're a good worker, Tucker. I'll get your pay." Butch wiped his hands again as he walked into the office. "That'll be fifty cents a tire."

Tucker smiled mischievously, "The station gets a dollar fifty for each tire you fix. Why don't I get more?"

Butch threw his head back in a hearty laugh. "Well Tucker, I provide the space; I provide the tools; I provide the customers; I provide the materials. I think fifty cents is a good rate for you."

"Okay," Tucker agreed. "So I get seven-fifty for the fifteen, plus another fifty cents for the John Deere tire. That sounds great." It wasn't a lot, but it was his money. He earned it, and he could spend it where he wanted to. It turned out to be a good morning.

Chapter 19
All Things Blessed

Tucker stayed out in the workshop all morning. He measured the boards twice and cut them once, something his grandfather taught him. Standing back, he admired the lumber. The wood was beautiful just as it was, even before the sanding and finishing. Everything smelled of wood fiber and sawdust, perfume to Tucker's thinking.

Christy went home after Tucker pumped air in her tire to give Rosie her lunch. At one hundred forty-five pounds the animal's meal of pig pellets filled her, until supper time. Freddie stopped by to watch Tucker work, then hurried out the workshop door heading toward his mother's kitchen to see what she had prepared.

Tucker put the tools on the workbench, except for the saw which he hung back on its assigned hook. He knew if he were to accidently step on the saw blade, it could bend or even break. He never wanted a single tool to break or wither into rust and die in his care. They all seemed to have a life of their own. He thought it was because Grandpop had touched them.

Tucker had no watch, and his grandfather certainly didn't keep a clock in his oasis of creativity, but Tuck thought he could risk leaving the shop unattended. With the door securely closed, he ran around the house with Winkler's Grocery Store, across the street, as his destination.

"Hi, Simon," Tucker said as he entered the little grocery and variety store with his eye on the back, right hand corner. He walked through the store excited by all that the small space could hold. "Simon, it sure is great you have all this stuff. It's five miles to town. Some families don't have a car. Grandpop doesn't even drive. Uncle Jacob said you know a lot about marketing."

"Tell him thank you." Simon bowed a little from the hips. "I think he means knowing how to sell something, not what I sell."

"Oh." Tucker didn't know what marketing meant, and didn't have the time to ask.

"Can I help you find something, Tucker?" Simon had time on his hands. Nearly noon, the store had few customers.

"Thanks, Simon," Tucker said but kept his focus on the prize. "I saw something on the variety side of the store the other day."

"Okay, holler if you need something."

Tucker made a beeline to the back of the store. The display tables, covered with small rectangles, separated by glass dividers and filled with a variety of items, all lined up in long rows. He wasn't shopping, however. He knew exactly what he wanted and which sparkling bin it was located in. He reached to the back of the display table and picked up a piece of purple cloth. Opening the yard of fabric, he held it out in front of him. *I'll make the present fit the fabric.*

"Ready?" Simon smiled as the boy neared the check-out counter. His expression changed, however when Tucker placed the purchase item on the counter in front of him. "Velvet? Tucker, you want to buy some yard goods? Velvet? Oh, I get it. Mrs. Moyer sent you over. What's your grandma going to make?"

Tucker thought for a moment. Should he tell Simon he was buying it for himself? Not to wear. It was to line something special in Uncle Jacob's gift. But … he didn't want to bring up the project. He thought again and wondered how many of his thoughts contained the word, *but*. He discovered already that there were two sides to most issues. Still, he didn't want to lie.

"It would make a fancy pillow, wouldn't it?" Tucker answered truthfully.

Simon raised his eyebrows. "It sure would, if you like velvet pillows."

"Carolyn does." Tucker put one dollar on the counter for the yard of fabric.

Simon smiled sympathetically. "With the bias tape, that will be $1.05. I can put that on your grandmother's bill if you want."

"No," Tucker answered quickly. Hesitating, he added. "I'll bring the five cents over later today. Can you wait?"

"I know," Simon perked up. "I think I'll be pretty busy on Thursday morning with people picking up last minute things for their Fourth of July picnics. How about you come over in the morning and sweep the front porch and steps. We'll call it even."

"Thanks," Tucker beamed. "See ya then." It was nearly noon. Tucker heard Gramma call for him to come in for lunch. "Gotta go."

"I heard her, too," Simon said with a smile.

Tucker gathered up his small sack and darted out the door. As he burst out into the sunshine, he shouted, "Coming Gramma."

The road was clear so Tucker ran across. This time, since food was involved, he used the front door. It was the shortest way into the house, directly across the street from the grocery store.

"What's for lunch, Gramma?" Tucker asked.

"Potato rivel soup," she said as she put a glass of milk at Tucker's place.

"Oh super. Will there be enough for supper, too?" Tucker slid into his seat, put his sack on the floor under his chair, and started to pick up his spoon.

"Hold on there, young man," Gramma cautioned. "Ya daresn't eat before you've washed your hands."

Tucker jumped up from the table and slipped into the tiny bathroom off the kitchen beneath the stairs. Even though it was small, it was in the only place Mr. Newton could find to put it when Grandpop decided to bring the plumbing into the house. Tucker reached for the Lux soap then remembered the radio advertisement, Lux: The Pure Beauty Soap Bar. Another bar on the shelf, still it its wrapper, was Grandpop's bar of Lava, the Pumice Powered Heavy Duty Hand Soap. Tucker decided, hard work meant serious clean-up. He pulled back the paper and scrubbed his hands with the rough, deep cleaning bar.

Betsy walked behind Tucker's empty chair, reached underneath for the sack, and then swooped into her spot at the table opposite Tucker's official seat. Her place at the table was a hold-over from earlier years when Tuck was compelled to kick his sister all through meal time. "Beat ya," she gloated as Tucker returned to the table. "Tucker," she mocked. "What's this?" Betsy waved the sack over her head.

Tucker gasped. Standing up, he grabbed across the table as Betsy jerked the sack back and forth out of his reach. "Gramma!" he yelled.

His grandmother continued to place bowls of soup at each place. When she got to Betsy, she leaned over her granddaughter's shoulder and spoke very clearly. "Betsy, give Tucker his sack. Now!"

Pouting, Betsy slumped back in the dining room chair. "Here," she threw the sack to her brother like she was pitching a baseball into home plate. "What is it that's so precious?"

Tucker put the velvet under his chair again. "Never you mind about what it is."

"How's the project comin'?" Grandpop sat at the head of the table, his official seat for the last fifty-six years.

"Project?" Betsy's eyes grew large. "What project?"

"Grandpop," Tucker complained. "Keep her away from it."

Grandpop touched Betsy's hand with his gnarled eighty-five year old finger tips. "Now Betsy, this is important to Tucker. Ya daresn't go into the shop until after the fifth of July. It's Tucker's project but it's my workshop. Stay out."

"Yes, Grandpop," Betsy agreed. She was a scamp* but she did obey Gramma and Grandpop. She played boys' games and encouraged Tucker to join in the fun. When Tucker was younger, she had to take him down and sit on him to get him to play field-lot football. But … she would stay out of the workshop. Grandpop said so.

"I'm about a third done with it." Tucker answered as he put his spoon in the steaming soup.

"Not, Tucker. Grace first," Gramma reminded him.

Grandpop closed his eyes and bowed his head. "Our kind heavenly Father, again we return thanks to thee for the privilege of being permitted to surround this table blessed by thy bountiful hands. Bless this food to its intended use. Fit and qualify our hearts to thy service. … And inspire Tucker with his project. In Christ the Redeemer's name. Amen."

"And, Lord, please keep Joe safe wherever he is," Tucker whispered.

"And, bless our friend, Joe," Grandpop added with a wink.

Everyone at the table ate in silence for a few minutes. The sound of Tucker's spoon scrapping the bottom of his bowl broke the treasured quiet.

"More soup, Tucker?" His grandmother started to push her chair away from the table.

"I'll get it, Gramma," Tucker volunteered as he jumped up.

"Ja, it's gut." Gramma settled back in her chair and smiled at her hot soup. "Don't scoop off all the potatoes and rivels."

Tucker returned to the table with his bowl in hand. "I didn't. They are the best part though." He smiled as he stuck his spoon in the soup again. It had tons of potatoes and triple the rivels. It was a warm July day but the soup warmed his innards* and Grandpop's prayer warmed his heart.

Chapter 20
Half Done is Half Not Done

"Tucker!" Betsy called from just outside the workshop door.

"Don't come in," he shouted back. "What ya want, Bets?"

"I'm going over to the vacant lot and see if there are enough guys around to get up a baseball game." She pushed the door open a crack and started to peek in.

"Elizabeth McBride," Gramma barked as she came up behind Betsy. Gramma carried a few cookies wrapped in a tea towel. "Your granddad told you to stay away from his shop."

"Yes, Ma'am," she agreed. "I just didn't want to leave Tucker out of a game."

"Right," Gramma's tone was skeptical. "Now, run along." She placed her hand on the door latch but waited until Betsy was out of the yard.

Tucker heard the latch opening and spread his arms over his project of golden wood. "Oh Gramma, it's you," he exhaled slowly.

"Thought you could use a few cookies," she said, looking over the many pieces of sawn and shaped wood that lay on the floor and workbench. "Rex Martin called and wants you to stop by the aircraft maintenance shop about five."

Tucker's eyes snapped to attention as he looked at Gramma. He nearly dropped one of the smaller pieces of wood he had been working on. Rex had promised to take him flying sometime during the summer. Gramma didn't know anything about it. "Oh? Did he say why?"

"No. Just save some time to see what he wants." Gramma handed over the fig newton bars, one of Tucker's favorites, and turned to go back to the house.

"Thanks Gramma," Tucker called after her. His mouth watered before he even took a bite. The two cookies buried in the tea towel looked really small, given that he could eat a whole package at one time. He decided to be thankful for the two since he didn't have to stop his work and go into the house to get them. Closing his eyes to savor each small nibble, he bit off a little of the golden cake surrounding the inner fig mixture and rolled it around in his mouth with his tongue. "Hmm," he whispered to the pointy awls* and the many sizes of screw drivers.

Again, Tucker licked his fingers and wiped them on his jeans before he touched the wood. The end grain was smooth where he had sanded away all the burrs and splinters. One of Grandpop's wide work pencils stood proud in an old coffee cup on the back of the workbench. Tucker grabbed it, the cloth, and the metal cased measuring tape. He studied the inch thick board, then measured off several trapezoid shaped cut marks along the end of the boards, and copied the same size and shapes to the longer ones. Grandpop called them dovetails and required a special short, thin dovetail saw. When Tucker cut the two long pieces and the two short ones, he ran his hand across the wood like he was petting Joe's silky coat.

One more long piece, Tucker mumbled. Hearing the directions spoken aloud helped him stay on task. More to the point, Tucker was a talker, hearing himself aloud helped him to concentrate. He looked at the big piece of lumber he had left and the pencil marks he made when he first measured everything. "That one needs to be fourteen inched tall," he concluded as he picked up the piece off the floor, "plus the wings and wedge."

Using his own muscles and his grandfather's crosscut saw, Tucker released the larger, fourteen by eight inch piece from the board, leaving two pieces, three by five inches. The remaining maple board was large. He could cut out four sturdy feet from it, and the piece that was on an angle for balance.

By supper time, all of the pieces were ready. Their surfaces, sanded smoother than the marble top on Gramma's tables, nearly shone. The slick dovetails had neither a splinter nor a split.

"Tucker," Betsy called from beyond the door. "Gramma said supper will be ready in a half hour and don't forget to check in with Rex Martin before we eat."

Tucker sized up all the preparations accomplished that day. Everything was ready for assembly and a high gloss finish. "Okay," he mumbled again. "I still have tomorrow to work, then a little time on the fourth."

Grandpop came out to the workshop just as Tucker hung the last tool on the wall. "How's it going, Tucker?"

"Done for today." He grabbed the straw broom Grandpop made last summer and swept up sawdust and small slivers. "I'm going to hurry over to see Rex Martin before supper. Tell Gramma I'll be right back."

"It's done for today, Tucker, but it's not done," his grandfather said softly.

"I'll have enough time, Pops. I know I will." Since it was summer, he knew it wouldn't get dark until about eight or eight-thirty.

Grandpop locked up his workshop and waved at the boy. "You daresn't be too long."

"I won't." Tucker's new bike, sleek and clean, was leaning against the side of the workshop when he came out. The handlebars felt strong and sound in his hands as he hopped on. Rather than biking on Route 33, he went past Aunt Franny and Uncle James' house and down around the corner, taking the long way around.

Bonzo, the Smeltzer family's Labrador, ran beside Tucker between Smeltzer's house and the next cross road.

The dog sneezed and sneezed, a kind of canine giggle, as it ran along with him. Tucker was familiar to Bonzo. The dog joined Tucker every evening when Tuck had filled in for Justin Smeltzer on his paper route last fall. Justin had the measles.

A mile over, around to the left, he coasted into the spot where Rex always parked when he was at the Midway Airport. Tucker pulled the front wheel into one of the slots on the bike rack and hurried in.

"Hello, Mate," Rex greeted with a broad smile. "Thanks for stopping. I was wondering if you'd get here before I locked up for the day. Polly is making fried chicken and corn on the cob for supper. I don't want to be late."

"I've been working on a project." Tucker looked around the space that always smelled like fine motor oil and airplane fuel. Every time Tucker smelled the aroma, it made him think of B-17 and B-24 bombers flying unescorted* missions he had seen in news reals at the movie theater, diving and maneuvering their way to victory. Also, the B-36 that flew right over his house came rushing into his mind.

Rex took off the crusty shirt he always wore when repairing engines and threw it over an old chair. "What project are you working on?"

Tucker hesitated a minute. "It's a secret"

Rex smiled as he patted Tucker's shoulder. "Then, I have another secret for you to keep."

Tucker shuffled from one foot to the other. "Another one?"

Rex chuckled as he guided Tucker toward the door. "You can do it." As he turned and locked up behind him, he winked. "I'll have the office open tomorrow, but on Independence Day, I want to take the plane up in the morning. I had some work done on it, and I want to make sure it's safe for our family flight on the weekend. You and I will buzz over to a nearby farm and repair another plane of mine. You always wanted to go up flying. How about it? Meet me at the airport at 10 in the morning?"

Tucker's insides jumped as high as the prospective airplane ride. *Someday is here!* "Christopher Columbus! Oh, wow, neat! Sure, I'll meet you at the airport. Why the secret?"

"Polly and the kids are so excited. I don't want them to get too wound up before I know if the plane is safe." Rex hopped in his car and started the engine.

As he pulled out of the parking space, Tucker hollered after him, "Okay, then … our secret."

Tuck hopped on his bike and pedaled toward home. His stomach grabbed his ribs as he pumped along, hoping he hadn't missed supper. When he got there, he turned in through the gate and pulled the bicycle up to the door of the summer house, before he darted in and swished through the kitchen.

"Well, there you are." Betsy's hands gripped her hips. "Did you go over to see Rex Martin, yet?"

Grandpop's eyes followed the two kids. "Tucker takes care of his obligations."

Tucker was glad Grandpop had interrupted Betsy. He now had two secrets to hold in his head and Tucker liked to talk. It was going to be hard, but mum's-the-word was going to have to be the operating practice. "It's a secret. I only have to keep it until the fourth."

"Rex Martin?" Betsy asked again. "What did he want?"

Tucker sat at the table and shifted his eyes from his glass of milk to his grandfather. Was Grandpop going to help him out again? "Well … I can't tell you."

"Oh, I get it …" Betsy mocked, "Another secret."

"Well," Tucker mumbled, "it *is* a secret."

"Yeah … right," Betsy mocked. "You are so full of fibs, Tucker McBride."

Tucker smelled supper as Gramma came closer to the table. She had a mound of crispy browned bacon, a bowl of scrambled eggs and a stack of toast made from her own wonderful bread.

"Now Tucker," Gramma warned, "I know you're hungry. You always are. So, take two spoonsful of eggs, no more than four pieces of bacon, and fill in the chinks with toast. There's more bread in the kitchen if there's not enough on the plate for you. You'll have to toast it."

"Thanks, Gramma," he whispered. He looked over at Betsy who kicked him under the table. He grinned a little because he knew that meant she was trying to keep the pecking order in line. After all, she was older, even if she was getting shorter. Tucker wanted to explain himself. He didn't want his family to think he wasn't telling the truth. What could he say? His project for Uncle Jacob's birthday had to be a surprise. It was special. And, Rex's secret was just that … his secret. Tucker couldn't tell anyone about it. It wasn't his to tell.

Chapter 21
Experiment One

Wednesday morning, Tucker lay in bed a little longer staring up at the ceiling. Usually his feet hit the floor as soon as his eyes opened, unlike Betsy and Tim. Gramma always said, "If it were up to those two they'd as soon turn the day upside down."

He tried to think about Uncle Jacob's present, but he couldn't concentrate. His thoughts bounced from hammocks, to velvet fabric, to his dad. He loved his new bicycle but couldn't decide how he felt about his father. *Boys love their dads. What's wrong with me? I don't want to be a taker or a hater.*

He finally got up while it was still early, just like his grandfather. Jeans he'd worn for two days lay on the floor. He pulled them on along with a white, high pocket T-shirt, and found some socks under his bed that smelled okay. He put on his heavy, high-top clodhoppers, ran the laces through the eyelets at the ankle, and tied them.

Downstairs, Tucker could see Grandpop through the kitchen window, weeding the garden. Gramma wasn't puttering through the house, tidying and straightening up. It was Wednesday; a little light cleaning was always on the schedule. *I won. Got up first!* He wondered if Gramma were sick but quickly decided not to think about that.

Tucker didn't really feel like talking. He had too much other stuff on his mind. He didn't go out to the garden to talk to his grandfather. Grandpop would be picking thin blades of grass out of the tomatoes. He wouldn't want to interrupt his fun.

Taking one of Gramma's small mixing bowls out of the kitchen cupboard, he filled it with his wonderful cereal and milk. Carrying it through the house to the porch, he was thankfully it didn't spill. He felt blessed by the luck of his Irish side when the heavy, etched glass front door opened without a squeak.

Out on the wide covered front porch, he sat on the wooden swing his grandfather had made. Suspended by strong chains, it had lasted since his mother was a child. To Tucker, the covered veranda was like a separate world, away from everyone. Red roses, the fresh, sweet aroma of dew, climbed up the trellis in the little flower bed that ran along the side of the porch. No place was better than that.

Tiny sat on the gray wooden floor in front of him, wiggling and watching, twitching and sneezing. Tucker smiled. "I suppose you want to clean out the bowl."

He tipped up the large bowl and sighed a satisfied sigh— *Yum.* The sugar he'd added to the cereal also sweetened the milk. As he wolfed down the last several spoonsful of flakes, he stared at the movement across the street.

The neighborhood was waking up. Simon Winkler was as predictable as the chime on Gramma's wall-mounted Regulator clock in the hall. As it chimed exactly at seven AM, Simon unlocked the door to his grocery. Just then, Freddie pulled up to the store, spinning his bike wheels in the gravel near the road sending dust into the air. He jumped off and followed Simon into the grocery.

The road beyond the front porch buzzed with people on their way to work. Tucker watched the cars, one by one. A 1939 four-door Nash sedan made its usual trip into Elkhart, carrying Alfred Walters to Miles Laboratory where he repaired any machinery that could slow down the production of Alka-Seltzer.

Most people hadn't had a new car for a long time. When the country entered the war, car manufacturers converted their factories into making the products of war. Now that the war was over, a few 1946 vehicles were beginning to appear on the streets. Tucker had fun naming the newest models, not recognized by some. Desoto and Hudson were his favorites. Gone were the ahooga horns, replaced by more sophisticated, deep throated beep beep models.

Freddie came out of the store, hopped on his bicycle and rode across the street. "You're up early." Freddie stood at the foot of the steps, straddling his bike's cross bar.

"You, too." Tucker placed the bowl on the floor so Tiny could lap up the last of the sweet milk.

Freddie tapped the side of the cross-body brown leather satchel he'd thrown over his shoulder. "Mom needs five pounds of hamburger to make summer beef stick. She'll mix it up as soon as I get it home. It takes a couple days before we can taste the beef stick. She called Simon with her order yesterday."

Tucker smiled faintly. "When Joe was home, Gramma used to tie a note to his collar and send him over to Winkler's. Simon would fill the order, charge the stuff to Gramma's bill, attach the sack to Joe again, and send him back home." His memory began to overtake him. "Even a pound of hamburger arrived at the front door untouched. Joe was a great dog."

"I remember Joe," Freddie said. "A really special shepherd dog."

"Yep." Tucker's voice faded into an uncomfortable broken whisper.

Freddie stared at the ground for a minute. "I better get going. Mom needs this meat. See ya later." He walked his bike around the side of the house. Tucker could hear his loose chain rattle on his bike guard as he peddled away.

"See ya," Tucker whispered after Freddie was gone. He sat there a few more minutes, his insides torn up over the loss of Joe. Finally, he couldn't stand just sitting there any longer. The bowl was still on the floor; Tuck picked it up, went inside and returned it to the kitchen. Standing at the window over the sink, he saw his grandfather walking down the street toward Uncle Jerry and Aunt Cora's house. With as much as Aunt Cora loved her family and wanted to know each detail of life, Tucker knew Grandpop would be gone for a while. Tucker thought for a second about the morning. That was the problem. He only thought for a second.

He was getting itchy and wanted something to do to release the tension of being in the middle of good and bad. He remembered something he'd seen on a top shelf in the cellar, behind Gramma's jars of canned peaches. Tucker suspected they had been there for a long time. Probably since his uncles were boys. Gramma was too short to reach them. He darted down the basement stairs, snatched the box, charged back up the steps and out through the summer house door when he heard Gramma walk across the squeaky living room floor upstairs. Tiny followed on his heels, sprinting ahead, sitting and waiting, then charging ahead again.

Running across the back yard to the workshop, Tucker saw the Stuart house inhale the day. Darren Stuart darted out his back door and nearly ran toward his car, as their screen door banged. Mr. Stuart seemed to run everywhere. He repaired walk-in freezers. July was the month when no restaurant could wait to have their refrigeration fixed. Tucker made sure the box he had gotten from the basement, wedged safely under his arm, didn't slip.

The key to Grandpop's workshop was still deep inside the pocket of the jeans he had on the day before. He slipped it in the lock. "Are you coming in, Tiny?" Tucker stood back and bowed low like a butler at the front door of a mansion. Tucker always said, Tiny thought she was queen of the litter. Tucker only humored her.

Inside, the small shop still smelled like maple wood sawdust. Tucker pulled a claw hammer from its assigned spot and put the box on the workbench.

He eyed the anvil mounted on an old tree stump near the door. The heavy steel was no match for Tucker. He pulled the entire anvil and its mounting out a little so the pointed end faced the door.

Opening the mysterious box, he found shiny brass 22 rifle shells. He thought up the experiment weeks ago but couldn't see how he'd get away with it. While sitting on the porch thinking of Joe, he remembered the procedure to test his hypothesis. For Tucker, doing something exciting usually chased away pain. However, it drove away logic, too.

His grandparents didn't allow Tucker to fire a rifle unless an adult was with him. In the fall, he'd go hunting with some of the uncles. That day, he didn't have access to a rifle. That didn't matter. He had to determine that he could fire a 22 cartridge in a different way, by hitting it with a hammer. He was sure he was right. *I know this will work. I'll prove it.*

The 22 shell looked small on top of the anvil. It never occurred to Tucker that anvil shooting might be dangerous. He lifted the hammer and slammed it down, but it hit the heavy iron block, missing the bullet. When the hammer re-bounded off the anvil it spun the cartridge around facing it in the opposite direction. The reflex action slammed the hammer down again, firing the bullet. Tucker jumped when the bullet from his hammer-gun hit his right thumbnail.

Tiny yipped and cried as she chased herself around in circles. Whining, she rubbed her right ear in the dust, then the left one. The little dog rolled on the floor and covered her head with both of her paws.

Tucker dropped the hammer on the dusty floor and clutched his thumb to his chest. The pain was almost unbearable. It made Tucker so sick at his stomach he dry-heaved until his sides hurt. Carefully inspecting his finger, the jagged corner of the nail was sticking up and the thumb was bleeding. He knew he had to go in the house to wrap it up.

When he walked inside, Gramma was standing at the kitchen counter adding a little milk to her cup of coffee. "Hey there, Tucker." She eyed the boy carefully. "What's going on?"

Tucker knew his shirt had sopped up blood from his hand. He couldn't hide a blob as big as that. He also figured his face showed how much his hand hurt. The frowning he couldn't mask was enough to give him a headache. "I was using Grandpop's hammer." Tucker was telling the truth. He was most definitely using his grandfather's hammer. "Did you hear that bang? I jumped and hit my hand." *That was no lie,* he rationalized in his head. *I did jump and the hammer did hit my thumb.*

"Well, put some salve on it and wrap it up. Tucker, you'll have to be more careful." She sipped the coffee and smiled. "I have a few minutes. The ladies are coming for our quilting bee and Bible study shortly. "

"Thought they usually came in the winter time," Tucker said as he walked into the kitchen.

"Not this time. Since Howard and his fiancée are getting married shortly, the women voted to give the quilt we're working on to them. We have a little bit to go to finish it." Gramma looked into the kitchen. "Do you want some help?"

"No, thanks … I can tie it off." A small cabinet in the corner of the kitchen held a few first aid items. Gramma bought band aids in their tin at Winkler's Grocery. For larger bandages, she washed old worn out sheets, then tore them into strips. She rolled the strips and stored them in a tin box tea bags came in. Tucker opened the tin and took out one of the rolls. He tore off a length of the muslin, put some salve on the throbbing thumb and wrapped the cloth around it several times. Near the end of the piece, he stopped wrapping, tore the cotton about five inches up the long way, and then, using the thinner pieces, he tied the bandage into place.

He made a mental note: *Experiment number one of cartridge- firing: don't hit the bullets with a hammer. It's too unpredictable.*

Chapter 22
The Quilting Bee

"I'll help Grandpop get the room ready for the quilt stretcher," Tucker offered when he came in from the kitchen with a bandage on his thumb.

"How's that thumb?" Gramma was trying to straighten Uncle Jacob's magazines and newspapers he had saved and stacked on the bookshelf. Books arranged in no order or size teetered haphazardly on several shelves.

"It's okay," he brushed off her concern. "Do you want me to take all that stuff and put it on Uncle Jacob's desk?"

His uncle's large, piled-high desk sat in front of the window in the entry hall. Tucker called it *the untouchable desk* because no one dare disturb anything once placed on it. If something was missing, no one wanted to accept the blame for its absence. As Tucker saw it, putting some more things on top was not the same thing as removing something from it.

"Well, now Tucker…" Gramma thought for moment. "Do you suppose there's room for anything else?"

He studied the desk again and wondered how he was going to pull that one off. "I've got an idea," he finally settled it. "Grandpop put a box into the hall storage closet at the church. The last order of church bulletins came in it. I could run over and get that box, put all the magazines and papers in it and store the box in the keyhole under the desk. That way, I won't touch the desk top at all."

"That is cleaver, Tucker. Ja, go get the box." Gramma beamed.

Tucker suspected she was embarrassed about the messy desk sitting right at the front door. She usually directed company to the smaller side porch entrance.

In his usual run to accomplish most tasks, Tucker flew out the side door, took the steps two at a time, and bounded across the street.

"Where ya goin'?" Freddie asked as he coasted his bike into the church's parking lot.

"Just picking up a box for Gramma," Tucker answered as he pulled the long handle on the church door.

Freddie followed him into the wide hallway and stopped inside the door, listening to the silence. "My foot, it sure is quiet in here."

"Yep," Tucker laughed. "No people, no music… no Anna Fredrick."

"Anna?" Freddie looked down at his shoes.

Tucker dropped the subject of Anna Frederick. He decided his suspicions were right. Freddie liked Anna. Tucker wouldn't want someone to tease him about a girl. "The box is in here." It really didn't matter to Tucker; it was just something to say that didn't involve Anna.

"What's it for?" Freddie asked.

"Gramma has some stuff to store." Tucker said no more. He opened the storage closet and pulled the box off the shelf. He quickly turned to start toward the door, wanting to make the sitting room respectable before the ladies came to work on the quilt, and have a short Bible study. With Independence Day coming up fast, there was a lot for Gramma to do.

Freddie stepped outside. "I'm going down to the creek after a while. Want to go?"

"Sure, Gramma is having the quilting bee at the house. That'd be perfect, as long as she doesn't need me." He ran across the street and up the steps. "See ya soon."

Inside, Grandpop had already moved Gramma's little rocker into the parlor. He was just pushing his Morris chair out of the way when Tucker jumped in to help. "Here Grandpop, let me help you with the couch." Together, they pushed the green striped couch into the parlor.

"I'll get the sawhorses; you get the quilt stretcher." Grandpop hurried into the kitchen and down the few steps into the summer kitchen. The wooden A-frame sawhorses he built for Rebecca to stretch the quilt across were stacked against the wall.

Tucker went over to the corner of the dining room where Gramma had leaned the quilt, which still spanned the stretcher. Long slats were attached to each end of the quilt by C-clamps Grandpop had brought up out of his workshop. At the quilting bee, several of the ladies from the church worked on the bright coverlet with woodland appliqués. They rolled the completed section on the top slat and released the last of the quilt from the bottom slat. Like the end of a scroll, the last few inches waited for the women to complete it. Howard and Pauline would certainly enjoy the beautiful needle work the ladies had for them.

"I'll make some fresh coffee." Gramma walked into the kitchen and filled the pot from the pump in the sink. The kitchen pump also was a Myer. The Myer clan was part of Gramma's distant family. When there was a knock at the door, she called out, "Tucker, please go to the door."

Tucker opened the door wide. "Come in Mrs. Peters. Gramma's making coffee." Before he closed the screen door, his Aunts Cora and Franny came up the sidewalk. Birdie Kline was right behind them. "Come on in," Tucker said with his usual broad smile.

Mrs. Kline paused at the door and looked Tucker in the eyes with a small *I-know-you* kind of look. "Have you found any more snakes?"

The smile on Tucker's face turned to a *caught-ya* expression. "No," he said slowly with a sheepish grin. He hung around a little longer just in case cookies were involved. Earlier that day, he snuck into the kitchen and searched Gramma's cookie jar and the bottom of the mop bucket in the storage cabinet, the usual hiding places for Gramma's homemade cookies, and found nothing.

Amelia Peters took her purse into the dining room and placed it on the table. "Did any of you hear that loud bang this morning?"

Aunt Franny's eyes opened wide. "I sure did. Howard said it was a gun shot."

Tucker heard that remark. He thought if he waited much longer, someone would get around to asking him if he heard the shot. He didn't want to lie. "Gramma," he started toward the door. "I'm going out to the workshop."

Chapter 23
Run Away Home

Back in Grandpop's workshop, it was early afternoon when Tucker finished assembling the pieces. Standing back, he smiled. It was turning out pretty good. He ran his fingers over the smooth wood. Now, the whole thing needed a high gloss finish. He searched Grandpop's shelves for a can of shellac. There it was.

Tiny jumped and wiggled around Tucker's feet. "Dog," Tucker commanded, "sit." Tiny folded her hind legs under her, sat down and watched.

Tucker checked the window opposite the door and made sure both were open as wide as possible. The workshop with Grandpop was a classroom for Tucker. Ventilation when using shellac was lesson number seven. He wiped the piece down with a clean tack cloth. With a small brush, he spread a thin layer of the shellac on every surface. It surprised Tucker when the whole room began to smell like alcohol. He immediately thought of what Gramma had said. "Now, Tucker, don't you drink alcohol. You could lose your senses." Tucker wondered if he'd start staggering or babbling if he inhaled more of the fumes.

He stepped outside the workshop and stared up into the big tree. Tiny didn't go outside until Tucker moved. The little dog followed, sneezing and shaking her head. Tucker would love to say Jacob's present was done, climb back up into the tree, and slide back out toward the hammock, if it was there, which it wasn't. *Escaping again?* He scolded himself. *Oh, no you don't. You're gonna finish this.*

Tucker took another clean tack cloth and wiped down his new bike. If he had to wait for the shellac to dry for twenty minutes, he'd make good use of his time. He was thorough, from the tire spokes, to the spot behind the chain guard, to the white wall tires.

Checking the Mickey Mouse watch he pulled from his pocket, he went back in and added another coat of shellac. He had to fill the ten minute break with something and get fresh air at the same time. He pulled a carrot from the garden and wiped the dirt under his arm on his shirt. Tiny jumped around him, yipping and dancing.

He was glad Grandpop found the Mickey watch with the broken band in the church parking lot the evening before. He checked it when the shellac went on and checked it again after another ten minutes, when it was time to add a third coat. He pulled Grandpop's key from his pocket and locked up the workshop for a while. He wanted no one to sneak around while he took a break.

Looking at his watch again, he saw that he still had time to meet Freddie down at the creek. After all, it was July. "Tiny," he ordered, "go find Gramma."

The little dog looked at him, her pointy ears twisting and moving in the direction of the boy's voice. "Yes, Tiny, go find Gramma."

When the little ball of fluff turned and headed straight toward the house, Tucker jumped on his bike, rode down the next street, and stopped in front of Christy's yard. She was sitting on the pale green glider on the porch. Her head was down reading the novel, *Black Beauty*.

"Hey, Christy," he called. When she looked up, he added, "Freddie and I are going down to the creek. Want to come along?"

"Sure." Christy opened the screen door and shouted into the living room. "Mom … I'm going down to the creek. I'll be home by suppertime."

From deep inside the house, Tucker heard, "Okay, Christmas."

Tucker saw Christy roll her eyes. He noticed that her mother insisted on calling Christy by her full name. It was a good name … a wonderful name. Tucker had to agree, *Christmas* was a rather formal name, a festive name. How can a girl play baseball or swing across the creek on a rope with a name like Christmas Tree?

He pedaled slowly as Christy jogged along beside him. Rosie trotted behind her. Tucker was surprised how the pig was able to make pretty good time. She raced along, not missing a twist or turn. It was only another block to the woods where Tucker would park his bicycle. "Come on," he said as they headed toward the high trees that lined the creek bank.

To Tucker, the creek and surrounding woods was one more spot on earth that resembled the Heaven he imagined. The breeze blew more gently there and the grass smelled sweeter, like a wet lawn following a rain.

"Hi, you two," Freddie called from the other side of the water. "Excuse me … you three. Who will be the first to fall in?"

The creek was wide and about four feet deep. At the center was an island or raised sandy spot, then it slopped to the lower part where the cool water waited. The idea was to swing out on one of the ropes that Tucker and some of the other kids in the neighborhood hung from branches of the trees. Two of the ropes hanging there were faded from years in the sun. Tim and his friends hung those years ago. Tucker would use the lower rope to climb up in a tree on the other side of the creek and swing out. If he missed the bank coming back, he'd drop into the water.

Christy grabbed the rope and swung out across the water just as Rosie's short little legs flew out and into the creek below. She splashed and grunted and, if it were possible, Tucker thought she smiled. Christy laughed so hard watching her pig's love of the water, she fell in. They all joined in the laughter.

"Hey, Christy," Ben Sherman called from the path. "Lightning and I will pull you out if you want." As he rode his horse closer, Tucker noticed Ben's eagerness to help.

"That's alright, Ben." Tucker shouted back. "I can help her."

"Oh you can?" Christy asked as she pulled her soaking wet body up out of the creek along a path in the bank and stood by Tucker.

"It looks like you can take care of yourself," Tucker laughed as he put his arm around Christy's shoulder.

"Hey, Tuck." Ben eased himself out of the saddle and slid to the ground. "Do ya want to ride Lightning?"

"Sure." Tucker always wanted an opportunity to ride a horse. Sometimes Gary Straum offered him a ride on his Chestnut mare when Uncle Jacob went for milk at their farm.

"Just remember, don't turn her north," Ben reminded him as he waved his finger at Tucker. "North is heading her home and she'll think it's time to eat."

"Okay," Tucker was so excited, he listened but didn't hear. He had one thing on his mind, riding the copper-red sorrel.

As he started to put his foot in the stirrup, Tucker ran his hand over the soft but coarse horse hair and mane. He could feel the mighty muscles under the thick skin or hide. Mounting Lightning, Tucker leaned near the soft spot that felt like fur behind the mare's ear. She smelled like new mown hay.

Tucker leaned into the saddle as he guided Lightning up from the bank of the creek. He rode straight and proud, like a western hero would sit astride his own mount. The day couldn't have been brighter or the sky more blue than what the Lord spread above his head. He touched the horse's side lightly with the heel of his shoe and advanced into a gallop. He imagined himself in the pioneer old west, riding into town, a man of mystery. He sat *tall in the saddle*, just like John Wayne. He turned on Moyer Avenue and galloped toward his home, in the direction of the highway. The sound of hoof beats and the crackling sound of the old leather saddle sang a duet to him as he rode along. He wanted to show off his riding ability. The problem was, the direction he was going was north.

Tucker's cousin, Luke, was riding in a friend's car just as Tucker got within a few blocks of the house. Lightning's gate doubled as she neared the highway. Beyond Route 33, the railroad tracks stretched out northwest and southeast. Tucker saw Luke's friend, Nathan, buzz past him, speeding for the tracks. Everyone in the neighborhood was aware that Lightning raced for the barn when pointed in that direction.

Tucker knew he'd be in trouble if Lightning reached the tracks and didn't stop. In his frenzied ride he saw the Lone Ranger leap over the tracks by flying in through the open door of a freight car, whisk all the way through and out the other side. This time that fantasy wasn't going to happen.

Car production had increased since the war was over. Companies shipped automobiles all over the country. Chevrolets rode on caged cars on that stretch of tracks. Tucker pulled on the horse's leather reigns so hard, he nearly toppled over backwards. Still, the mare didn't respond but fixed her target on the big red barn behind Sherman's farm house on the other side of the tracks.

Nathan's wheels skidded in the gravel at the edge of the tracks and threw small rocks into the air. Luke slid from the seat beside him and slumped to the floor. Finally, Lightning reared back and pawed the air while Tucker held on to her mane and enjoyed the excitement of her amazing stop.

Tucker's cheeks hurt from grinning. "Well, that was a fast ride."

"You ..." Luke yelled as he brushed himself off. "Doesn't anything scare you?"

"Sure," Tucker laughed. "But, it isn't you." He smiled inside and out, as he remembered, *I've got the joy, joy, joy, joy down in my heart ...*

When he looked around he saw Ben running after him and Lightning, his arms flailing at his sides. "Look back there," Tucker cracked as he threw his leg over the horse and dismounted. Freddie ran up the street following the entire band of horse wrestlers, while Christy pumped along on Tucker's bicycle. Rosie waddled behind them.

"What ... time is it?" Freddie gasped, doubling over as he tried to catch his breath.

Luke brushed himself off and checked his watch. "It's five o'clock."

"Five?" Tucker's mouth popped open. "I gotta go." He dashed back up to the highway with Christy and his bike behind him. At the first break in the traffic, he darted across the street. "See you all tomorrow."

Running through the side yard he laughed and jumped for joy. The excitement of the ride was addicting. The silky dog flew off the side porch, yipping and yapping, to join in the fun, following Tucker to the workshop.

Tuck bent down and scratched Tiny's ear. "Did you see me, girl? What a thrill!"

"Here's your bike, Tucker." Christy breathed heavily as she jumped off the Schwinn.

"Thanks, Christy." He doubled over, still laughing. Then he stood up as fast as Lightning had stopped. "Oh no." Tucker stopped and caught his breath. "Did Lightning make me lose the key?"

"I'll bet it's still there." Christy encouraged him.

He fished deep in his pocket and felt something hard. "It's Grandpop's workshop key." He smiled and raised his eyes to Heaven, kissed the skeleton key, and then stuck it in the lock.

"I'm going on home. See ya later." Christy waved and ran out of the yard in the direction of Franklin Street.

Inside the workshop, the project still smelled of alcohol from the many coats of shellac he rubbed on it earlier. The wood was smooth to the touch. The can of maple wood stain that he had gotten out was still on the workbench. With a clean tack cloth, he rubbed the rich color of maple into the wood and sealed it with another layer of the orange shellac. Its amber tone brought out the natural red in the wood. The beautiful, completed piece looked warm. Tucker stood back and looked at Uncle Jacob's present with pride … but … enough of that. He was hungry.

Chapter 24
Tucker Explains

The house smelled like the cornmeal mush Gramma had cooked for breakfast a few days back. She always made sure she prepared a lot of the thick, hot pudding. After breakfast, she poured the leftover mush into a loaf pan and put it in the ice box. During supper time preparation, while Tucker was still in the workshop, she sliced the loaf of chilled mush like a loaf of bread and fried the pieces in rich butter in her favorite cast iron skillet. The fried mush filled a platter with rectangular patties. The plate arrived at the table just as Tucker finished washing his hands.

The second Grandpop finished the evening grace Tucker reached for the butter and slathered it on three thick pieces he had put on his plate. On top, he poured sweet, woody, warm maple syrup. Tucker smiled to himself as he poured the golden tree juice on the mush … a maple syrup reward for a maple finish on his project. Since he wanted the project to remain a secret until tomorrow, he could tell no one of the prize he had created.

"What are you grinning about?" Tim teased.

"Who me?" Tucker felt his face grow hot, and began to wiggle and shift. "Nothin'." But Tucker managed a knowing smile. He let Tim know, perhaps there was a secret, but he wasn't going to talk.

"How was your day?" Gramma asked. She had seen all the help he had given and the project he had worked on. Indeed, Tucker had been working hard that day.

Carolyn brushed her shinny hair from her face. "And … why were you late for supper?"

Tucker looked up from his plate. Everyone was looking at him. Were they actually going to listen to him? "Well, I worked in Grandpop's workshop most of the day. Then I went down to the creek with Freddie and Christy. We swung across the creek several times. Christy fell in. I didn't." He put another bite of fried much in his mouth and went on. "Then I rode Ben's horse a little but Lightning got away and ran for home." He became more excited and animated as he relived the story of the runaway mare. "There was a train on the track but I got her stopped before she crashed into the side of one of the cars. Then I went back to the shop and finished my project."

Carolyn rolled her eyes, sat back in her chair and folded her arms.

Tim blurted out, "Tucker, you are so full of it."

Betsy glared at Tucker with eyes of steel. "Come on Tucker. No one wants to listen to your tall tales."

Gramma reached over and patted Tucker's hand. "So you finished your project, Tucker. That's wonderful. I'm very proud of you."

"Thanks Gramma," he whispered. He saw his brother and sisters grit their teeth but said no more. Tucker smiled a toothy grin and wished he had more fried mush.

Chapter 25
Remembering

After supper that same Wednesday, Tucker wandered out onto the side porch. He tried to think of something exciting and uniquely his to do. The sky was still crystal blue without a trace of clouds. A welcomed breeze chased away the heat of the day. Overhead, birds were singing from the top of fruit trees and from inside thorny blackberry bushes. It wasn't time to go in for the evening. Evening hadn't started yet. It was July and it would be daylight in northern Indiana until about eight o'clock, but somewhat different from the rest of the country. Indiana saw no need to embrace Daylight Savings Time. Indiana's eight was Ohio's nine. Tucker's favorite radio programs wouldn't be on for hours. Now, what to do?

Gramma came hurrying out of the house, handbag in hand and hat on her head. "Tucker, Uncle Jacob is taking Aunt Cora and me over to the supermarket in Goshen. We'll be back in an hour. Stay out of trouble. Your grandfather is napping. He'll probably wake up in a few minutes."

"Yes, Ma'am," Tucker said, shifting from one porch step to another as he watched Uncle Jacob and his grandmother get in the car, pull out of the drive and head toward the Lehman home. Just then, he heard the screen door bang on the heel of Tim's shoe.

"I'm goin' out, Tucker," Tim announced as he bounced down the steps. "I'm meeting friends at the Burger Drive-in."

"Right," Tucker sighed.

"You okay?" Tim asked as he turned and eyed the boy up and down.

Tucker's head was down studying a colony of large black ants in the crack in the sidewalk where the concrete met the steps. "Sure," Tucker responded weakly.

"No, you're not," Tim snapped and rested his foot on the bottom tread. "What's going on?"

Tucker's voice drifted off. "I was just trying to see her in my mind. I...don't remember Momma, Tim. What was she like?"

"Of course you don't, Tuck. You were a baby when she died." Tim folded his hands over his knee and leaned in toward his brother. "Well, she was very pretty with dark wavy hair just like yours," he began with a smile.

Tucker watched as Tim's eyes beamed with happy memories. Tuck could easily see how much Tim remembered and how much he missed their mother. Tucker had only one memory. "I remember a lady getting me dressed when I was real little." He smiled mischievously. "I peed all over my clean clothes," Tucker blurted out. "Gramma said the lady was mother."

"That's a good memory," Tim began slowly. "Let's see, Mother was creative like Carolyn, and active in everything around her like Betsy," Tim explained with a smile. "She had a canary," he remembered with a chuckle. "Every morning Mom would come into the living room and say, 'Good morning, Bobby. Do you have a song for me?' The bright little bird would sing the whole time Mom was fixing breakfast."

"Wow," Tucker breathed out in amazement. "I never heard that story before. Why?"

"I don't know. I'm sorry I never told you." Tim flipped his keys in the air, a cue that he was leaving. Then he added. "There was a grape arbor in the backyard of the little house up the street where we lived. Mom pressed and canned all the grape juice the church needed for Holy Communion for the entire year. She was a good person." He paused and nudged Tucker's knee. "I never told you, but…she would have been proud of all the stuff you make and the creative ideas you come up with, even the crazy ones. What made you think of Mom all of a sudden?"

Tucker shrugged and slumped back with his elbows on the step above him. "I've been mad at Dad lately, and then I realized I hadn't even thought about Mother. I wondered if she thought I didn't care"

Tim didn't say anything for a minute. "She knows you love her, Tucker. She didn't live long enough for you to have memories of her." He straightened and added, "She didn't want to leave you. She just died. Dad didn't die, but he doesn't seem to want to spend much time with us either."

Tucker wiped his nose on his sleeve. "Family is a funny thing, isn't it?"

"Yep, it sure is," Tim agreed. He started to turn again. "Hey, Tuck, can you keep a secret?"

"Sure," Tucker looked up, wondering what Tim had on his mind.

"Well," Tim began as he looked to the right and left.

It looked to Tuck like Tim was checking for those who might hear.

Tim whispered, "I should be getting my draft papers soon. The war is over, but they still need guys to help secure and clean up Europe." Again, his eyes searched the yard for someone who might be lurking around a corner or hiding behind a tree. "Jim Straighter and I want to join the Marines, not the Army. Tomorrow is Independence Day, but on Friday, we're going into Goshen to sign up for the Marines before we're drafted and won't be able to choose the branch we want."

Tucker's heart pounded as he grinned. "You're going to be a Marine?" Then Tucker's face darkened with a mix of pride and fear. "Almost twenty-five thousand Marines were killed in the war, Tim. Tons more in the Army and Air Force."

"The war is over, Tucker," Tim said as he threw his head back. "Now, shush." He winked at Tuck and added, "So much for keeping a secret."

Tucker laughed, "No, no. I won't tell anyone until after you sign up." He threw his arms out wide. "Then, I'll tell everyone!"

"Great. I knew I could depend on you." Tim turned and started for his 1937 DeSoto two-door sedan parked in the drive. "Gotta run. Gonna meet Jim for a burger and a malt."

"You just ate," Tucker called after him, reminding him of Gramma's fried mush.

"You know me. I can always eat." Tim jumped into his car and started the engine.

Tucker sat for another moment, nearly bursting with an avalanche of pride, secret keeping, and the sad awareness that his family would soon change again. He knew his dad wasn't in the military during the war, but he wasn't sure he was ready to give his brother over to the military generals just yet either. The more he thought about it, the more his pride fought it out with a fear of losing another family member. "Can't think about that right now," he demanded of himself.

If Joe were here, Tucker thought, *we'd go down by the creek and skip some pebbles. Joe would take a swim. But, Joe isn't here. Mother's not here, and soon, Tim won't be here either. Like Gramma said, I need do something instead of giving in to the feelings I don't want, feelings that just make me feel awful. What can I do?*

Tiny pushed the bottom of the screen door with her head and wiggled her way out onto the porch. She got down on all four paws, crept over to Tucker, and nudged the boy's arm to gain a cozy position leaning on his thigh.

"Hi, Tiny." Tucker sat there rubbing the little dog's tummy and stared across the street. "What can we do?"

Tiny wiggled out again and scampered over to a tree near the sidewalk. She bounced up and down, scratching at a round green thing shaped like a baseball.

Tucker picked up the hedge apple and searched it for insects buried in the bumpy surface. "Oh, you want to play catch?" He brought the Osage-orange to his nose and inhaled the citrusy aroma. "No," he said with a firm laugh, "I am not going to take a bite."

Prancing and bouncing, Tiny backed up toward the tree like an outfielder going deep to make a catch. When her boy didn't toss the hedge apple in her direction, she announced her impatience with a single yip.

"Okay, okay," Tucker said with a roll of his eyes. "I have a better idea." He got down near the grass under the medium-size thorny tree and searched for more of the yellow-green, grapefruit sized fruit, or hedge apples as Uncle Jacob called them. With the bottom of his T-shirt stretched out in front of him, Tucker loaded his *work-apron* with seven or eight of the funny-looking, nearly inedible fruit.

Balancing the large balls, he ran around to the summer kitchen door, slipped in, and hopped down and around the corner to the basement. He had seen spiders and their webs when he was down there earlier. The hedge apples would be the right thing to chase them away.

With the precision of an insect exterminator, Tucker placed a hedge apple first in the two corners of the basement window ledges, and the back niche of Gramma's fruit shelves. The other four he spaced around the concrete walls in a balanced pattern.

Behind the furnace, where the large asbestos-wrapped trunk line fed from the coal boiler to the heat lines of the house, Tucker saw something he had never noticed before. How was that possible? He thought he knew every inch of the house, from the basement to the attic.

Then he remembered something Grandpop said. "You have to use tools properly to be safe." Grandpop went on with an example. "I remember when your Uncle James was about your age. I had to take a bow and arrow away from him. He was shooting at the tops of corn stalks before the tassels had dropped their pollen. I told him to stop it. I planned to give it back after he learned his lesson. But…I forgot where I put it."

Tucker smiled to himself. *Uncle James' loss is my gain.* The hedge apples seemed to call to him from the corners. Grinning, he bounded up the steps with the bow and quiver in one hand and Tiny yipping at his heels from behind.

Gathering a half-dozen more hedge apples from under the dense, flexible hardwood, he smiled. The hedge apple was the perfect tree for making bows and arrows, and for hiding them, too. He whisked the cockroach-chasing "apples" around to the corner of the yard near Grandpop's workshop. Behind and beside the shop, running between the alley and the grass, his grandfather installed a picket fence some years back. Tucker lined the hedge apples along the top rail of the fence and stood back.

With long strides, he then paced off ten yards back from the target, pulled an arrow from the quiver, and aimed it slowly with the close of one eye. The arrow made a thwishing sound when Tucker released it, followed by the twang of the string. It wooshed toward its target and hit the first hedge apple with a thunk. "Yeah!" Tucker yelled in victory.

"Yeah, what?" Christy called from down the alley. "Whatcha doin'?"

He lifted the bow over his head in triumph and laughed. "I hit it … the hedge apple!"

"Wow, where'd ya get the archery set?" Christy came into the yard and inspected the pierced target.

"Found it in the basement."

"Does your grandmother know you have it?"

"Well…no. She's not home. Uncle Jacob took her to the grocery."

"Hmm." Christy thought for a moment. "Aim a few more times, then you'd better put it back. You know your grandma."

"Right." Tucker did know his grandmother, very well, and Christy was right. "Okay, a few more," he said as he positioned the bow and arrow again.

"When will she get home?" Christy asked just as Tucker released the arrow from his bow again.

As was his nature, he turned in the direction of Christy's voice, away from the target. He didn't hear a thunk. The sound he heard was a thud and a flat tweet.

"Tucker!" Christy gasped, grabbing her mouth. "You hit an American goldfinch."

"What?" Tucker moaned. "A wild canary? No!"

"Come on," Christy urged as she ran to where the bird had fallen.

The bright yellow song bird with the black forehead and wings fell to the ground in the dust of the alley. Tucker just stood there for a second, then bent down and rubbed his fingertips over the soft wing feathers. Tears ran down the boy's cheeks and dripped from his chin as he sat beside it in the rutted drive.

"Bobby," he whispered. "Do you have a song for me? Sing…please, sing to me."

Christy put her hand on Tucker's shoulder as he sat there in the dust. "Don't worry about an arrow hitting one bird, Tuck. My dad said, to end the war, it took just two bombs to kill a couple hundred-thousand people in Japan." She tried to help Tucker see the larger picture.

"But, this isn't the other side of the world, Christy. It's the other side of the yard," he insisted as he rubbed his eyes. "And, this was my mom's little bird."

Tiny ran over and sniffed at the finch. She nudged the bird with her nose. Suddenly, the wild canary's wing fluttered and it hopped up on its skinny, stick-like feet.

"Tucker," Christy's eyes bulged and a smile spread across her face. "The bird isn't dead. The arrow must have stunned it and knocked him out of the sky."

"But…how…?" Tucker couldn't believe his own eyes. Joe never came home. He might as well have died. "How could a little bird fall out of the sky and—"

Christy's voice softened. "Mrs. Kline said the Bible tells us, 'Are not two sparrows sold for a penny? Yet not one of them will fall to the ground outside your Father's care.'"

Tucker shook his head. "How did you remember that?"

As Tucker watched, the Bobby bird expanded its wings and took to the air, soaring and dipping. From a tree limb, safely off the ground, the wild canary began to sing the sweet song of hope Tucker had asked for.

Tucker felt the song bury itself in his heart and knew his mother was near, smiling. He had solved his doubts about his mother, the parent who was gone, and his fear that she knew he hadn't remembered her. Now, he had to solve the doubts he had about his father, the parent who lived only a few miles away. If Joe had come home, maybe he could have solved his feelings of a broken, incomplete family.

Chapter 26
An Unfortunate Noise

July 4, 1946

Tucker didn't stop for breakfast. He'd made a deal with Simon. He grabbed Gramma's broom out of the closet and ran out the front door. Not wanting to look like a warlock on a broomstick, he held it in both hands above his head as he darted across the street.

Winkler's Grocery hadn't even opened yet. Tucker saw Simon's car approaching and figured he must be coming in early to prepare for last minute holiday shoppers.

With the energy of a twelve-year-old, Tucker swept the concrete porch and steps, not missing a leaf or a twig, just as Simon pulled his car around to the back of the store. When Tucker finished, he stood back and admired his work.

"Looks great, Tucker," Simon said as he came around to the front of the building and inspected the job. "You've earned a coke on top of your nickel. Come over anytime and collect."

"Thanks Simon." Tucker hoisted the broomstick again. "Gotta run."

"Good job," Simon called after him. "See ya later."

Tucker slipped in through the front door, replaced the broom where it had hung from a closet nail, fished the cereal box out of the cupboard, and was sitting at the dining room table, tipping up his bowl of Kellogg's flakes when Freddie knocked on the screen door. "Hi, Freddie," Tucker greeted him but didn't open the door. According to his grandmother, she preferred kids take their fun outside, not bring it in the house.

Freddie shielded his eyes with his hands so he could peer in through the screen on the door. "Can ya come out? Bring your BB gun."

"Why does Tucker need his BB gun?" Tuck's grandmother asked.

Freddie rubbed off the brown smudge from his nose where he touched the metallic smelling screen. "It's the fourth of July. My father said we could shoot out into the vacant lot. Get the fun started. The war's over."

"Kinda early isn't it Freddie?" Tucker's grandmother questioned. "It's only seven fifteen in the morning. Some late-night workers are sleeping since they have the day off."

"Our house is on the edge of town so we'll shoot out back toward the open field." Freddie stretched back up as Tucker came to the door.

"I know where you live." Gramma looked at him square in the eye. "Will your father be home?"

"Yep ..." Freddie gulped. "Ah sorry, yes ma'am."

"Well, okay then. It is the fourth of July ... is it not?"

Tucker was excited. His insides jiggled as he charged up the stairs, two treads at a time. Fishing around under his bed, he smiled. *Yes!*

He rummaged through his sock drawer and dug out a red, cardboard box of Daisy BBs and several packages of roll caps. Fast as he could, he yanked out two full heavy paper rolls and stuffed them in his jeans pockets. He started to leave but went back for the third roll in the box. Darting out his bedroom door, he ran smack into Carolyn in the hallway.

"Watch where you're going, little brother."

"Little? Look whose calling someone little." He waved the third roll of caps at her, to make a more powerful point. "You're no taller than Gramma."

"What's that in your hand, Tucker McBride?" Her hands were on her hips like they always were when she used her *I'm responsible for you* voice.

"Never mind. Gramma knows." He slipped out of Carolyn's reach and bounded down the steps, jumping with a thud to the floor by leaping over the last four treads. He called the wide jump, *bailing out.*

"Grandma," Carolyn called as she leaned over the bannister. "Tucker has his BB gun and a bunch of BBs and caps."

Gramma was sitting in the living room, enjoying a second cup of coffee. She raised her voice barely above a whisper. "I know Carolyn. Thank you for watching out for Tucker. You're a big help."

Carolyn said no more but glared at Tucker.

He hit the screen door running, leaped off the side porch, made an amazing landing, and ran off with Freddie. The weather was perfect. Not a single cloud dotted the sky. Even though it was still morning, it was already getting hot. Tucker hoped the temperature would get in the high eighties. It was July after all. Three years before it was ninety-one degrees on the fourth of July.

"You have your BB gun, and I have my cap pistol." Freddie's voice sounded excited, and then his tone seemed to droop. "Wish I had a BB rifle."

"You have that corn field behind your house, right? That's where we're going to shoot? Do you have a target set up?"

"Yes ... yes ... and no," Freddie said, teasing. "I didn't think about a target since my cap pistol won't actually shoot anything."

"That's okay." Tucker was still flying high with excitement. As they neared Freddie's house, Tucker sized up the possibilities. "We could get on our stomachs and shoot through the balusters on the front porch like a snipper."

Freddie wrinkled his nose. "What's a baluster?"

Tucker liked knowing something a friend didn't know. "Grandpop just repaired some of them on our front porch. Balusters are the posts that hold up the top railing around the porch."

"Oh, okay, I know what you mean." Freddie puffed out his chest. "Dad sanded the handrail after Mom got a splinter in her hand. The handrail is—"

Tucker interrupted a silly statement. "I know, Freddie. It's the rail where your hand rests as you go up the steps."

Freddie didn't say anything, but then added. "We'll shoot from the chicken coop in the back yard."

Tucker grabbed Freddie by the arm. "You've got chickens in that coop haven't you? I was pecked on the top of the head by a crazed chicken one time and don't want to be attacked again."

"These chickens are nice," Freddie insisted. "You're so active and fidgety, maybe they wonder when you're going to be on the move again."

"I didn't know chickens wondered…about anything." Tucker followed Freddie as he stepped over the board at the bottom of the coop door. Inside, Tucker's sinuses hit a confused mix of smells. Clean straw covered the hens' nests. Stale feathers floated everywhere. Loose ones fluttered to his shoulders. He tried to brush them off but new ones only replaced them. The offensive odor that crawled into his nose and pounded above his eyes was the fumes coming from the droppings scattered on the floor. "Oh, pee-yew."

"You'll get used to it," Freddie assured him. "Don't even think about it."

Tucker wished he had something to shove up his nose so he'd have to breathe through his mouth and by-pass the olfactory* sense. But…he didn't. He fussed for a moment, and then coached himself…*Never mind.* He shook his head and focused on the space. "Over there are some windows, no glass, nothing will get broken."

The windows were pretty high, making it hard for them to stick their guns out the openings so they would be able to aim their shots properly. "Here, help me," Tucker took hold of the end of a simple wooden bench and motioned for Freddie to grab the other end.

Freddie hesitated. "That's Mom's bench she sits on when she's sorting out the sick little chicks from the well ones."

Tucker sighed loudly. "We're not going to wreck it, Freddie. We're just going to stand on it for a little while. We'll put it back."

His friend studied the bench for a moment. "Okay, okay. Let's get it over in place. Quick, before I change my mind."

Together they moved the crude bench over beneath the windows, hopped up on it and stuck their weapons out the openings. Instantly, in Tucker's mind, he was on the catwalk of the wall above the Alamo, defending the Texas Territory fort with his long rifle through the firing hole. Davie Crockett and James Bowie fought beside him on the bench as the three defended the fort. **POW, POW** the gun announced.

"I have a better weapon," Freddie suggested as he jumped down and picked something up off the floor wrapped in one of his mother's hand embroidered pillow cases. He slowly pulled off the linen. "It was my great-grandfather's civil war musket. Muskets were still used by some soldiers early in the war."

"Wow," Tucker gasped. "Does your dad know you have that?

"He's sleeping in his chair beside the radio. I didn't want to bother him. He doesn't like it when I wake him up." Freddie pulled his handkerchief from his pocket and wiped the musket carefully. "Dad showed it to me the other day and let me hold it."

"Oh, okay," Tucker agreed. After all, one introduction, one touch, opened the door to a new and exciting relationship with the musket. "Well, Mr. Crockett, what do we do now?"

Freddie looked from the weapon in his hand to Tucker whose mouth was gapping. "Do we fire the canon?"

Tucker looked around the coop. Again the scene changed. He was now completely unaware of the chickens or their smell. The scent of musket powder hung in the air. He was defending the fort. "What canon?"

"This one," Freddie sighed and rolled his eyes up to the feather coated ceiling.

"Oh, right," Tucker nodded as he inspected the hundred year old weapon.

"Okay, let's test the canon first." Freddie put a cap under the hammer of the old musket and pulled the trigger. *Pop.*

Tucker's shoulders slumped. "That wasn't much." He pulled the complete roll of caps from his pocket. That was the roll he grabbed at the last moment. Now he was very happy he had.

"Great," his friend nearly giggled. Freddie stuck his hand deep in his pocket and out came a roll of something Tucker had never seen before. "Dad brought home some of this new electrician's tape. I have an idea. Here, help me. If one roll isn't enough, we'll try more." He handed the tape to Tucker.

Freddie folded the paper cap roll carefully, centering one percussion cap over the one under it. With the musket in hand, he pulled back the hammer. "Tape the caps right under the hammer."

Tucker was so giddy over the ability of the two frontiersmen to guard everyone within the fort by firing the cannon from the catwalk high above the surrounding fort wall, he nearly dropped the tape. He pulled off a long strip and held it in his left hand. After several attempts, he placed the caps properly, like any experienced sharpshooter.

"You fire your gun and I'll fire the cannon," Freddie ordered.

Both of the defenders placed their weapons in position, ready to fire with the seriousness of a major battle. Tucker fired the BB gun, aiming at one of the fence posts on the corn field line. *Pop*, he hit it dead center. Freddie pulled the trigger of the old musket, prepared to strike the stack of caps. Magnified by the small chicken coop, there was a loud ***Kaboom*** and a flash of fire. When the hammer struck the first cap, it ignited the others making them all explode.

Tucker's ears rang like someone had turned the theme song from *The Lone Ranger* up at full blast.

Neighborhood dogs howled in every yard close to the boys' battleground. Tucker heard the sound of pain in the canine howling and completely understood. The flash and the ear thumping sounds, all trapped within the walls of that very small chicken coop, caused both boys to fall from the bench and land in a heap.

At that moment, Tucker remembered the chicken droppings on the floor, some dry and some gooey. He jumped up, brushing himself off all over. "I gotta go home."

Freddie stuck his finger in his ear and shook it fast. "What?"

"Gotta go," Tucker repeated. He grabbed up his BB gun and ran out the rustic door. His ears rang so loudly, the ringing blocked out all other sounds. If Freddie said anything more, Tucker didn't hear it.

As he ran toward home, he wondered how far the sound carried. Maybe showing up in the living room with a Daisy BB gun in his hand was not good timing. He raced in through the alley beside the yard near Grandpop's workshop. Pulling his grandfather's shop key from deep in his pocket, he opened the door and started to stash the gun in the corner. That spot did not hide anything. Looking around for a better hiding place, he reached up and pushed the gun onto one of the boards above his head where Grandpop stored rough lumber and other things.

Relocking the door, he walked down the alley to avoid the yard. Perhaps meeting Rex at the airport without going back inside the house would be the better plan. Riding his bicycle over to the airport was out of the question. He had parked the bike near the side porch and didn't want anyone to see him just yet. He stuffed his hands in his pockets, walked through the back of the church parking lot and started toward the airport, away from the house.

Wonder what time it is? Then he remembered the watch in his pocket. Tucker knew Rex wanted to take off for the blue sky yet that morning. Then, there was the Moyer family picnic at noon. The fireworks were set for sundown. Mickey's yellow gloves pointed to a *better hurry* time, so he ran all the way, a little over a mile, not wanting to be late for anything. Tucker saw Rex getting out of his car. *Oh good, I'm just in time.*

Chapter 27
Up and Down the Celebration Day

Tucker followed Rex out to the runway where a mechanic was bringing up the airplane. As it rolled to a stop, the aircraft looked bigger than Tucker remembered. Or, maybe it just looked larger on the ground than it did in the sky.

Rex patted the door and twisted the handle. "Since it's the Fourth of July I want to get over to Nappanee early enough to repair the other plane and get home by lunch. I have to fix the rudder cable on the smaller airplane so a friend of mine can rent it to go on vacation."

Tucker wasn't sure about the rudder. He loved airplanes but didn't know the vocabulary yet. "What happened to the rudder?"

Rex shook his head in disgust. "I loaned that airplane to another friend. He clipped a cement fence post on take-off and broke the rudder cable. The rudder helps to turn the plane."

Tucker nodded in agreement. "So, you can't fly without it."

"True," Rex agreed and quickly opened the door. "Well, Tucker, let's get in."

Rex climbed into the Ercoupe and maneuvered himself over behind the controls. Tucker got in the co-pilot's seat and buckled up.

"Gee, this is super," Tucker looked it over, from corner to cranny*, every knob, dial, and gauge. His instinct was to touch everything but thought better of that. He could easily touch something he shouldn't since he didn't know what the knobs were supposed to do.

"This flight will be short," Rex assured him as he started through the pre-flight checklist. "And, it is safe. Life Magazine described this aircraft as 'nearly foolproof.' They even had pictures of a pilot landing his plane with his hands over his head. I can do that."

With Rex's hands not in the air but on the controls, Tucker heard a high pitched buzz as they started to taxi down the dirt airstrip. Tuck could feel the vibration from the revved up engine, like a thoroughbred horse kicking at the sides of the starting gate. Releasing the brake, the plane lunged forward while gaining speed. The dashboard rattled as they bounced down the runway. Tucker's heart pounded with excitement as the coup cleared the ground and lifted off. When they were airborne, Rex turned the craft southwest toward Wakarusa and banked due south in the direction of Nappanee.

The view from above was exactly as Tucker imagined. Green corn stalks lined up in rows like a company of Army cadets. Well maintained farm ponds sparkled in the sun, always waiting to provide water to cattle and relief in case of fire. Coming to the farmer's pasture where they would land, Rex made a circle and came into the field due east. Landing, Rex throttled down and taxied to the end of the field where a fence marked off the orchard from the corn and circled, heading the plane west again before they stopped.

Rex powered the engine down in a whirl. "Okay, Tucker let's find that rudder cable. You can help."

"Hi, Sam," Rex called out to the man in overalls who walked toward them. "You're just lucky I was able to come this morning. I have my right-hand assistant with me. Sam Hall … meet Tucker McBride."

"Hello there, young man," the farmer said as he offered his hand. "Are you in airplane mechanic school?"

"Sure, I want to learn all Rex can teach me." Tucker was usually an active talker, but when he was near Rex's airplane he just wanted to stay quiet and learn. He wished he could tell his family about all he had taken in, but they either wouldn't believe him or they'd keep him closer to home. More secrets.

Rex handed Tucker a shiny U-bolt. "You hang on to this until I ask for it."

"Sure," Tucker agreed with pride. He was definitely going to assist.

Rex removed the inspection plate on the rudder and checked the cable. Sure enough, the cable was broken. "Okay, Tucker, hand me that U-bolt."

Tucker clutched the bolt tightly in his hand. Handing it over, he smiled inside. He felt like he was really assisting.

Rex spliced the two sections of the cable in the Cessna 172 with the bolt, closed the plate and rubbed his hands together. "Done," he announced.

"That's all there is to it?" Tucker gasped. "We had to come all the way over here to put in a U-bolt?"

"Yep," Rex agreed. "It's my plane. I'm the mechanic. I want to fix it myself so I know it's done right."

"Good idea." Tucker beamed. The warmth of his grin puffed out his chest. He was part of a team that started a job, stuck with it, and finished the whole thing.

"Okay, Sam." Rex threw both hands up. "I'm done. You and your family enjoy your trip."

"Thanks again, Rex," Sam said as he beamed. "The family would be really disappointed if we weren't able to take the trip we'd planned."

The sun was high overhead, with brilliant streams of golden light bouncing off the pond to the west of the farm house. Tucker couldn't wait to be in the sky again, flying like a bird to his nest. It was getting close to lunch. Without even looking at his watch, his stomach told him it was mealtime. He thought of the juicy hamburgers Uncle Jacob would make. His uncle had spent part of yesterday removing all the grass and leaves from around a shallow hole he had dug. Then he stacked rocks around that pit. Today, he would fill the hole with coals, then lay a metal rack across the burning embers to grill as many meat patties as the family could eat. Tucker could smell them cooking and taste their smoky deliciousness as he climbed back in the Ercoupe.

"Buckle up," Rex said. "Let's hurry. Fried Chicken is waiting. Polly will be at the airport, ready to take you back home and me to the dinner table."

Again, Rex revved the engine and held the brake tight to get the RPMs up for take-off. As soon as he released the brake, they shot down the bumpy pasture and lifted off. Airborne, they climbed instantly to 60 feet. Suddenly, in the blinding glare of the sun off the pond, a radio tower loomed up ahead. Instantly Tucker blurted out, "Tower!" He grabbed the co-pilot's wheel at the same time Rex realized the danger and responded … but it was too late.

Images of Mrs. Kline teaching his Sunday school class flashed through his mind. "Remember class," she warned them all. "To be men and women of God, honesty is the first thing you need to practice in order to succeed."

Vivid mental pictures of home flashed before his eyes. He remembered stories of people drowning, going under the water for the third time. The music of Gramma's warm teachings and visions of Grandpop's wrinkled but strong hands as he braided string into rope on the front porch tumbled and rolled before his eyes.

With a jolt and loud thud Tucker saw the right wing tear away from the fuselage. The force spun the plane around like a helicopter blade.

They descended in a whirl and pancaked in a teeth-rattling crash on the ground. Tucker heard ripping, tearing and grinding as they flattened, belly down in the dirt. Thrust forward at great force, Tucker hit his forehead on the instrument panel. A welt formed immediately. He knew he'd go home with a bump and a bruise. He felt like an angry stork had snatched him up in his bill, leaving the baseball bruise on one side of his head and the bump from the dashboard on the other.

Rex quickly flipped the master switch shutting off all electricity. "Get out … get out now!" Rex yelled. It all happened in a matter of seconds.

Tucker didn't ask questions. He was the one to spot the tower. His aching head told him they hit it. He was out and away from the cockpit in a flash.

Tucker and Rex stood back several yards in case the airplane exploded sending shrapnel everywhere. In the continuing blinding sun, they saw that the left wing now bent under and the propeller bent backward toward the engine.

"Wow!" Tucker exhaled, releasing all tension. He realized they had just survived a major airplane crash.

Sam Hall ran across the field, hopping and limping. When he reached them, he bent over from the waist, out of breath. "Are you two all right?" he gasped.

"Yeah, I think so. We hit pretty hard. Glad we're alive." Rex shook his arms and stretched out his legs. "You okay, Tucker?"

"I'm fine." Tucker said nothing about his bump. He usually complained to no one about anything. That wasn't his style.

Rex reached out to touch the boy's forehead. "Looks to me like you got quite a lump coming."

Tucker shrunk back from his touch. It hurt badly, but he wouldn't give in to the pain. "I'm okay."

Sam put his hand to his chest and tried to catch his breath. "I told Maude to call Polly. She should be here soon and take you guys home."

"Polly can take Tucker back." Rex's face was set in firm determination. "I'll stay here and help load the Ercoupe on your hay wagon. We'll take it back to the airport where I can work on it."

Tucker thought for a second. "What about your chicken dinner?" His stomach gurgled at the thought of the rest of the food that would go with the meal, like buttery mashed potatoes and milk gravy. He hadn't even had his morning snack yet.

"Lunch will still be there when I get home. Right now I have to get my plane back to the shop."

Tucker jumped at the chance to have another adventure. "I can help you load it. I'd be happy to."

Rex smiled at him. "Your grandfather told me how strong you are. But, I'm not going to get on the wrong side of your grandmother. You'd better get home. Do you want Sam to call her and tell her what happened?"

"Good grief, no," Tucker gasped. He didn't think Gramma would want to hear what had happened. "It's better that we don't bother Gramma." Then Tucker remembered. "She has high blood pressure you know."

"Oh, okay," Rex agreed. He glanced at Tucker. "Sorry, things changed. This trip was a dud for you."

Tucker slapped Rex on the shoulder. "No dud, Rex. It was real jake. It couldn't have been better."

Chapter 28
The Picnic was no Picnic

Polly Martin pulled to the sidewalk at the side of Tucker's house. "Thanks for helping Rex, Tucker. He told me you actually kept him from having a more serious accident. He said you grabbed the controls and pulled the two of you away from the radio tower. For that, I really want to thank you."

Tucker liked those words. It was nice someone recognized that his help was important. "Thanks, Mrs. Martin."

Polly put her hand on the car's door handle. "Do you want me to come in and explain what you did?"

"No, thanks." Tucker wasn't sure what he was going to tell everyone. From what he saw of the backyard, the family had been there for a while. Some of the cousins were laughing and playing croquet. The pattern of croquet wickets was stuck in the ground out across the lawn near the garden.

"Oh no," Tucker heard a rookie yell from the third wicket. He figured a good player sent someone's ball *home*.

Tucker slipped in through the side door and looked around. Gramma and Grandpop sat in *their* chairs chatting with those around them. Betsy and some girl-cousins headed upstairs, giggling like always. He figured they wanted to talk about boys. Over at the table, there was still a lot of food left. He was especially glad there were plenty of hamburger patties on the platter. He worried the hamburgers would be cold by that time. It looked like Gramma had placed the hot water bottle under the plate. Touching one of the burgers with his finger, he found it was still warm. The potato salad bowl was half full of potato bites, hard-boiled eggs, onion and celery. Gramma had already dished up a wonderful tapioca pudding into small cups. He knew he'd have to take five or six of the cups to have even a little of the tapioca he'd normally eat.

"Where have you been?" Carolyn questioned with her hands anchored as always. She eyed Tucker up and down. Reaching out, she touched his forehead gently. "What happened to you?"

The welt above his right eyebrow had turned into a large knot. The bruise had spread wider with red, blue and yellow colors seeping into it. "Ouch," Tucker flinched, surprising himself.

"Tucker McBride," Carolyn looked intently at the wound. "Where have you been? Where'd you get that thing on your forehead?"

Tucker could always depend on Carolyn to look after him. But, her extra mothering was hard on his need for independence. She was one more person who tracked him around the neighborhood. "Tucker … you answer me."

"I was in an airplane wreck," he blurted out without thinking. He wished he hadn't spoken and closed his eyes tight, gritting his teeth. *Couldn't I have come up with a more likeable story than the truth?*

"A plane wreck?" Her voice cracked and her eyes flashed.

It was easy for Tucker to see how angry Carolyn was. No one could miss it. Everyone could see it on her face. They certainly heard her. By that time, everyone in the house had lowered their voices.

Gramma steadied herself as she got up and hurried over to the buffet table with her index finger to her lips. "Why are you yelling?"

Carolyn closed her eyes, shook her head, and lowered her voice to a tight whisper. "Sorry Gramma…but Tucker just lied to me."

Gramma's face fell into disappointment. "Lied to you?" She turned to the boy. "Well, now Tucker, what's this all about?"

"Gramma," Carolyn interrupted with a hoarse whisper, "Tucker said he was late because he was in an airplane crash." She turned to Tucker and glared. "An airplane crash? You could have told a more believable story than that."

Those sitting in the living and dining rooms turned toward Tucker and shook their heads in disbelief. "More lies," someone said. "That's Tucker," another cousin mumbled. "He's always saying something to get you riled up."

Tucker heard the words clear down in the pit of his stomach. He didn't like the feeling. Still, that wasn't going to keep him from eating. He looked at the table loaded with food. It all still looked really good. Maybe his stomach discomfort wasn't embarrassment after all. Perhaps it was just hunger.

"Get some food, Tucker," his grandmother said as she patted his back. "We'll talk about plane wrecks later. You daresn't go anywhere though. In fact, stay in the house until we get to the bottom of this."

"Okay, Gramma. That's okay." As long as the tapioca held out, Tucker would be happy to stay inside. He placed three cups of tapioca to the side while he filled his plate. A hamburger bun piled high with meat, onion and catsup took up a prominent one-fourth of the plate. Next, he added potato salad, baked beans, and Aunt Cora's homemade pickles. He took everything and found a spot under the dining room table to sit and eat. From his vantage point he could watch the whole family. Those standing closest to the table were easy for him to hear and follow their conversation.

"What was Carolyn talking about?" he heard Uncle Jacob ask Gramma. "Sounded like something about an accident."

Tucker was glad he'd found a place at the dinner table, or actually under the table. Always aware of what his family might think, he wondered if they would decide he had gotten under the table so he could eavesdrop on other people. That wasn't his plan but he had to admit, it worked quite well.

"Carolyn was complaining something about Tucker lying to her," Gramma whispered. "A bunch of nonsense about Tucker being in an airplane crash."

"Crash?" Jacob gasped in a hoarse whisper. "Does he look hurt?"

"Well, now that you mention it, yes." Her eyes widened. "He had quite a bang on his forehead." She stepped aside as Aunt Cora came back to the table for second helpings. As she walked out of earshot, Gramma added, "I wondered where that bump came from?"

Betsy and the girls came downstairs after hearing all the raised voices declare Tucker a fabricator of fantasies. Standing to the side of the table, Betsy reached between Gramma and Uncle Jacob to grab a stalk of celery. Munching on the green treat stuffed with peanut butter, she couldn't keep quiet. While she loved to tease Tucker from time to time, she was always the first to stick up for him.

"Sure, Grandma. Don't you remember when Rex Martin called the other day? He asked Tucker to come over. I never asked Tucker what Rex wanted."

Jacob looked around the room for those who might listen. "Polly Martin brought him home," he whispered.

Gramma put her hand to her mouth. "You don't think…"

Chapter 29
Trust but Verify

Jacob slipped out of the house while the rest of the family enjoyed each other's company, and walked to his car. Since he was still young, healthy, and had a good job, Jacob was the one responsible for his sister, Margie's children. He was their legal guardian. If one of the four was involved in a serious accident, he had to check into it.

The small local airport was just a little south on Route 33. The family passed it every time they went to Goshen. The Midway "airport" was a simple half-mile dirt runway for small airplanes. Businessmen in Elkhart County used the landing strip for quick business trips and weekend vacations. Several times Uncle Jacob had taken Tucker and Betsy down to see a new plane come in. Sometimes it was an Ercoupe, other times a Beechcraft, or a Cessna.

Once at the airport, Jacob looked around before getting out of his car. Then … there it was in his rearview mirror. Behind him a farm tractor pulling a hay wagon turned into the field and moved toward the hanger. Jacob was stunned. His mouth flew open as he watched a wrecked Ercoupe bounce along the path on the bed of the wagon. As they passed, Jacob saw Rex Martin sitting on the end with his feet hanging over the end. Jacob followed the tractor, moving in closer when the hay wagon pulled inside the hanger.

Rex jumped off. "Hi there, Jacob. What are you doing down here on a holiday? Tucker said you were having a big family picnic at your house today."

"I was just checking to see … if you were all right."
He didn't want to put words into Rex's mouth. Wanting to
be fair, he thought he'd let Rex tell the story, just in case it
wasn't the same as Tucker's version.

"Oh sure." Rex walked around, checking the fuselage
on all sides. "I'm fine. It was Tucker's side of the plane that
took the most damage. He's the one with the big knot on his
head." He had a wrinkled, tight brow when he stopped and
looked at Jacob. "How is he? I guess I was more concerned
about my airplane than my co-pilot."

Jacob felt awful. "Tucker doesn't complain. He
didn't say too much until Carolyn asked him. His grandma
and I just noticed it."

"That's Tucker McBride, isn't it, Jacob?" Rex
chuckled and shook his head. Then his tone turned more
serious. "You people can be really proud of him. He not only
saw the radio tower before I did, he grabbed the wheel.
When he jerked the plane away from the tower, it still tore
the right wing off, but there could have been even more
damage." Rex rubbed his hand across his forehead. "We
could have both been hurt really bad. He's quite a kid, isn't
he?"

Jacob felt the energy drain from his face and body.
Tucker had been in an airplane crash and no one at home
believed him. "Yes, he is quite a kid, Rex." He turned toward
the car without saying more.

Jacob drove home thinking about all the freedom
Tucker had around the neighborhood. During the summer,
the boy would leave the house after breakfast and not return
home until lunch. He'd walk across the highway back into
the woods and farmland that once belonged to his great-
grandfather. One day his hike led him to an old brick
foundation all covered with weeds. His grandfather later told
him his archeologic expedition uncovered the foundation of
the family homestead. Jacob had wondered how a twelve
year old boy could get into an air accident and no one even

knew he'd gone flying. He finally realized Tucker's home was everywhere his feet could carry him.

Chapter 30
Under the Table

From under the table, Tucker saw a pair of legs standing beside the plate of brownies one of the aunts brought. He recognized the shoes. They were Christy's white patent leathers with the little heels. He knew how much she liked the fancy new shoes so he decided they were okay. Still, how anyone could run bases in slippers with thin little soles and no shoelaces to hold them on, he couldn't understand.

"Here's a plate, Christy," Gramma offered. "Help yourself to the food. We'll have birthday cake for Tucker's uncle a little later."

"Thank you, Mrs. Moyer." Christy filled her plate with carrot sticks, potato salad with a homemade sweet tangy dressing, a chocolate chip cookie rich in butter and bits of pecans, and a thick hamburger on a bun. Loaded with cheese, onion and pickles it looked to Tucker from his vantage point like Christy's mouth drooled. She looked around at others in the room. Some kids were sitting on the floor in the corner of the sewing room playing Monopoly, but Tucker wasn't with them.

Tucker tapped Christy on her shoe, startling her so much, she nearly dropped her plate. "Christy," Tucker whispered from where he sat cross legged beneath the table. "Come down here. This seems to be the safest place in the house." He looked around at feet and knees. "Where's Rosie? She probably wouldn't be welcome in the house."

"I know," Christy agreed as she bent low. "I wouldn't dream of taking her into someone's house. Look out the screen door. She's waiting out there."

Tucker could see out the door between people's legs. There was Rosie by the hedge at the end of the sidewalk. As he watched, the pig sighed and flopped down on the cool grass. Tucker smiled remembering that was just what Joe used to do.

Christy gathered up her full, red and white striped skirt and stuffed it between her knees as she crawled under the oak table. She had tucked her blue top with white stars of various sizes into her waist band. Quickly, she grabbed the cookie to keep it from falling. She nearly added chocolate to her Independence Day outfit. "What are you doing down here?"

"Things were getting too … uncomfortable." Tucker finished off his plate of food but was still hungry. "Stay," he ordered Christy, jumped up and scooped up a huge helping of apple salad with raisins and marshmallows. He slipped back under the table balancing his plate in both hands.

"Stay?" Christy mouthed a silent bellow. "What am I, a dog?"

"Bow wow," Tucker teased. "A grand champion."

Christy smiled and changed the subject. "Rumor has it, you were in an airplane accident today, Tucker." Her voice sounded concerned. She ran the tips of her fingers gently over the growing bump on his forehead.

Tucker flinched. "Careful," he jerked back and smiled. "It'll be okay. The bump will probably be gone by tomorrow."

"Have you cleaned it off?" Christy kept staring at the bump that seemed to grow larger rather than smaller.

"You sound like Gramma," he teased.

Christy gave him a sideways glance and nudged his arm. "You mean I sound like I'm seventy years old … or, do I sound like I care if you get an infection?"

Tucker didn't say anything. He just smiled sheepishly.

Tiny crawled on all fours, inching her way under the table cloth and into the magic kingdom of Tucker.

"Hi girl," Tucker smiled and rubbed the dog's tummy.

Tiny turned in a flash and snatched Christy's half eaten hamburger patty off her plate. The silky had the browned meat between her front paws and protected it by hovering over it with her body.

"Get it," Tucker gasped, his voice going into gravel mode. "Gramma will be mad if she sees Tiny eating people-food. She'll be even more upset if she gets a greasy smudge on her carpet.

Tiny tried to protect her treasure, growling and twisting away. As the little dog wrestled with the meat, one of her toenails looped through a floral pattern in Gramma's lace tablecloth. Everything on the buffet table sat on that lacy masterpiece of needle art and it was sliding. Rolling around under the table, Tiny finally let loose of the hamburger just as the table cloth began to move even closer to the edge.

The first bowl to hit the floor was Aunt Cora's pickled cucumbers and onion salad. That was all right with Tucker. He didn't like cucumbers and onions mixed in vinegar, sugar and garlic any way. Now, however, the vinegar and water mixture was all over the floor.

Tucker shoved his plate in Christy's direction, thrust his hands up around the edge of the table and held on. Betsy ran over and steadied the food as the bowls and plates teetered near the edge. The fancy cut glass dish holding stuffed green olives was the last to go. Green eyes with red pimento pupils rolled all over the floor.

"Watch out!" Tucker yelled just as Carolyn's left foot came down on one of the juicy green ones. The cherry red pimento shot cross the room like a crimson, gooey cannonball.

Carolyn did a little side shuffle and missed the larger pile of cucumbers. However, she didn't miss seeing Tucker under the table. In fact, there were two under there. "Tucker … get out from under that table."

"Sorry, Carolyn," Christy apologized as she too crawled out from beneath the table. "It was the dog that pulled on the table cloth, not us."

"She's right," Tim agreed. Up until then, he had been quietly standing along the wall near the entry. "I was watching what that silly little dog could get into. I saw her get tangled in the lace."

Tucker followed Christy out of their hiding place. Looking at the spilled food, his shoulders fell.

"Never mind, Tucker," Tim offered. "I'll get some towels and clean up this mess."

"Thanks, Tim." Tucker was surprised. Like any older brother, Tim usually razzed him, not rescued him. With a rattle of the screen door, Tucker's attention was turned to Uncle Jacob as he jerked opened the side door and stepped in.

Jacob looked around the room, found Tucker and smiled. He went over and put his hand on the boy's shoulder. Everyone had stopped talking. The pale face and sober expression made Jacob look like he was serious. "Mother," he announced to Gramma and all those in the house, "we'd better take Tucker into the hospital. The injury to his head came when he was with Rex Martin an hour or so ago. Rex crashed his airplane and Tuck was in the co-pilot seat. It was because Tucker grabbed the wheel and jerked the plane away from a tower in the field that they weren't hurt worse."

A large gasp rose up from the family. Then, the room was quiet.

Chapter 31
The Present

Tucker's mouth dropped open. "How did you know about the crash?" Then he thought about the rest of Uncle Jacob's announcement. "I don't want to go to the hospital."

When the family heard Tucker mention the hospital, they all grew silent. Tucker was a tough kid. He almost never went to the hospital, regardless of his injury. Just like the bullet to his thumb, no one else knew. He didn't tell anyone what had happened.

"First, I talked to Rex Martin. Tucker, he said he crashed his airplane, but you grabbed the controls and maneuvered the plane so the impact wasn't as bad as it would have been. He said he was really proud of you, and he wants to thank you, a lot."

Tucker blushed and stared at the floor. He didn't think anyone would find out. If they did, he'd get into trouble for going flying without telling anyone first.

Tim walked past him carrying a tea towel full of olives. He paused by Tucker's side and gave him a brotherly tap on his shoulder. He said nothing but Tucker knew his brother approved.

Uncle Jacob raised his eyebrows. "As to the hospital, let's ask your Aunt Franny." The family always depended on Aunt Franny for first aid information and many more things of daily living.

Franny Moyer got up from the couch when she heard her name. "Glory be, Tucker, let's have a look." She brushed back the wave that covered the side of Tucker's forehead. There, like a coalminer's headlamp, was a bump as big as an egg. Thankfully, the bleeding had stopped. "It looks like you've cleaned it up."

"No," Tucker explained. "Polly Martin had a first aid kit along. The farmer's wife, Maud told Polly I'd gotten a bump and it was bleeding. When Mrs. Martin got there, she took care of it."

Franny studied the cut and bruise carefully. "Well, Polly Martin is a practical nurse. She doesn't work anymore, but she still knows her stuff." Franny touched the wound lightly and smiled. "It looks good, Jacob."

"Thanks," Uncle Jacob said no more.

Tucker knew his uncle was a quiet man. He talked a lot when someone asked him a question, but didn't often volunteer information.

Gramma put her arms around Tucker in a bear hug like he rarely got. "You could have been hurt worse, Tucker. Why didn't you tell your grandfather or me before you went up in the airplane, like we talked about?"

"Why? I wasn't going to pilot the plane." In a way, Tucker was right. The morning wasn't going to be anything he created on his own. He was just going for a ride with someone else in the pilot's seat. "Rex goes up all the time," he reminded her. "I was just riding along."

Gramma wiped a tear from her cheek. "You are absolutely right, Tucker. Thanks for reminding me."

He smiled and winked. "Another reminder, Gramma. When ya going to get out the birthday cake?"

Gramma took the signal. "Tucker, come help me with the dessert plates. You come too, Christy."

Tucker followed his grandmother into the kitchen. She had already placed small forks in a large spoon holder that had belonged to her Grandma Schaffer. Christy picked up the forks. Tucker saw a stack of small plates and retrieved those. Gramma brought in the cake that looked to Tucker like chocolate with fudge icing, his favorite. He figured Gramma didn't trust him not to drop it or run his fingers along the edge of the icing. Tucker and Christy followed her while she sang out, *Happy Birthday to you…"*

Oohs and aahs escaped all over the living room along with the birthday song as she placed the huge fudge cake on the table. Gramma turned. "Before I cut the cake … Tucker has something for Jacob."

Tucker hurried into the hall. Sliding on an oriental throw rug, he grabbed hold of the brass knob of the closet door. Down on his knees, he crawled into the closet, all the way to the back, and pulled out a large present wrapped in last Sunday's comic strip section of the Elkhart Truth newspaper.

He carried it into the living room and handed it to his uncle. "Happy Birthday, Uncle Jacob," he said with a broad smile of pride and appreciation.

"Goodness, Tucker. What do you have here?" Uncle Jacob's eyes brighten. He sat down on one of the dining room chairs and put the present on the floor. "I like your wrapping paper. It's very imaginative."

"Thanks," Tucker whispered, embarrassed.

Uncle Jacob pulled a small penknife from his pocket and slid it under the rough fiber rope Tucker had tied around it to hold the wrapping in place. With the rope cut, the paper fell from a highly polished, maple wood, open top box lined in purple velvet. It had dovetail joints at the corners and a dip fashioned in the middle of the front. It was about the size of a large shoe box but with higher sides and a raised back. Another deep pocket was over at the side.

"I bought the velvet from Winkler's Store."

"And, I bet you earned the money by fixing flat tires," Jacob said with a quiet smile. "This is really something."

"Do you know what it is?" Tucker grinned when he saw Uncle Jacob study the gift, turning it front and back.

Grandpop stood back with pride. "He worked on that for hours, over several days. Tucker never did tell me what you'll use if for."

Tucker's shirt nearly split. He was proud of his work, but in usual Tucker style, he was having as much fun stumping his family. Finally, he blurted out, "It's a violin holder*." Tucker slowly ran his fingers over the velvet. "Sunday evening, I saw you get out your violin and then have to put it back when you had to walk away from it, to keep Tiny from stepping on it."

"That is brilliant." Uncle Jacob studied the luster on the wood. "Your workmanship is amazing."

"Thank you." Tucker felt his cheeks get hot. He hadn't heard any of those words before. He shook off the embarrassment by talking. "With this holder, you put your violin down in the box part and lean it against the back. The bow goes in the pocket there on the side. Tiny can't knock it over when it's in the violin stand."

Gramma put her arm around Tucker's shoulder. "You're growing up, Tucker. You took on the project and worked until you were finished. Good job."

He looked around the room and smiled. Faces looking back at him were warm, and he had to admit, they usually were. He realized that families come in many clusters of folks … and this group was his.

Chapter 32
A Hero's Return

About eight PM it was growing dark as shadows merged and the last of a crimson glow slipped below the horizon. Grandpop had moved the two metal tulip chairs from the front porch to the back yard. He had painted them red last week just for this occasion.

Howard brought a few wooden folding chairs over from the church fellowship hall after the Independence Day parade late in the morning. "Only people over twenty-one can sit on a chair," he said with a joking laugh.

The family joined in his fun. "It was ninety degrees today. The ground's warm," someone added. No matter what Howard said, everyone was glad he was home from the Navy. Other aunts and uncles either dragged chairs from home or spread blankets on the grass.

"It's got to be warmer here than at our house. You're farther south than we are," Uncle David laughed. David and Aunt Karen came with their camp chairs and their children, adding two more cousins to the yard. They just lived in Elkhart, four and a half miles away, but it was a different world to Tucker. He wondered if, some day, he would be able to move more than a few blocks from Gramma and Grandpop.

The Moyer yard was the perfect place to watch the fireworks that would soon begin. The bursts of light would come from the high school baseball field a few blocks away. There was a good, wide pocket of sky above the family's garden where tree limbs wouldn't block the view of the explosions of color.

Tucker had a better idea, as he always did. The tree over the summer kitchen had that really keen low hanging branch that had served him well the other day. "Gramma," he whispered in her ear. There was no need for everyone to hear what he said to her. "Is it okay if I sit in the tree over there," he pointed to the corner of the house.

"Ja, Tucker … of course." She smiled and nodded toward the sidewalk. "Them, too."

Christy had gone home for a while that afternoon, to change her clothes, and to feed and pen up Rosie so she couldn't follow. Christy biked into the yard and adjusted the kickstand. Freddie was right behind her. "Good evening, Mrs. Moyer," the girl greeted. She wore some blue jeans cut off just above the knee and lace-up clodhoppers like Tucker's. Her top was a bright red T-shirt with blue and white embroidered stars around the crew neck. Freddie was dressed like Tucker in the uniform of the day … jeans and T-shirt.

"Come on," Tucker motioned, pointing to the upper branch. "Hope you can climb the tree, Christy. We'll get a better view up there."

"Fiddle de dee." Christy raced ahead to the tree and seemed to remember how Tucker had tackled the climb. She threw her left leg up over the limb above her just as Tucker had done. She too hung upside down from there until she could hoist herself up to the long, horizontal branch higher in the crook of the tree.

"Wow." Amazed, Freddie looked up at the tree again. "I can make it," he whispered to himself, but Tucker heard him.

"What's the matter, Freddie," Christy called back with a smirk. "Can't climb a little tree? I showed you how."

Freddie glanced over at Tucker as if he'd get some support from his friend. "I can climb a tree ya know. I just don't know if I can climb this one."

Tucker patted him on the shoulder. "Of course you can do it … leg up first. The rest will make sense."

Freddie smiled weakly. "Right." He aimed his leg at the limb but missed. "Now wait, just w-wait a minute," he stuttered. Swinging his leg back and forth a few times, he threw his heel up in the air with Tucker behind him pushing on the seat of his pants. "Whoa…" Freddie yelled as he bolted up to the tree limb. "Wow, what a kick." He looked at the next branch up and turned to the ground. "I think I'll slide over here." The first branch he landed on was the limb he decided to stay on.

Tucker figured Freddie wasn't going to risk the embarrassment of trying for a higher branch and maybe not make it. Once Freddie and Christy were perched in the tree, Tucker hoisted himself up beside Christy, using the leg over limb, upside down approach. The heat of the July day gave way to pleasant warmth as darkness overtook the yard, turning off God's super lamp in the heavens.

With the night sky soothed and only the twinkle of stars to lighten the area, Tucker caught a glimpse of Uncle Jacob as he walked out to the road and over to the church parking lot. Tucker hadn't noticed a car in the area. He'd been too busy talking and climbing. When did people in the strange car get there, and why did they come on a family night of exploding rockets? Tucker watched as Jacob approached the car.

As the car door opened, suddenly the night sky burst with the electrified boom and crackle of brilliant, multi-colored lights. The lingering smell of gunpowder hung in the smoke overhead, indicating the major fireworks were on the way.

Christy stared up. "I love the ones that fill the entire sky. The ones with many brilliant colors"

"Me too," Tucker agreed but he couldn't take his attention from what Uncle Jacob was doing. As the sky burst again with explosive sounds and flashes of light, Tucker could see clearly. Jacob was leading a big dog from the church to the yard. "Oh, please … but it can't be," he whispered to himself as he scrambled down to the lower branch, and then leaped to the ground from there.

Uncle Jacob released the leash, freeing the dog to run and bounce across the lawn. It looked like a mix of German shepherd, a full grown one, not a puppy. The animal's stride was too long for a frisky young one. Tucker walked slowly, mumbling to himself as he went. "Did Uncle Jacob get a new dog?"

"I heard you whisper, Tucker," Gramma said as she came up beside him.

Just then, Grandpop was at his side, too. "No, we didn't talk about a new dog. I suppose that would be nice though."

As Tuck got closer, he stared at Uncle Jacob and then the dog that ran in front of him. "Can it be?"

The animal had no answers, only action. He leaped up on Tucker with his front paws and slurped up love from his face.

"How?" Tucker cried as tears ran down his face and added to Joe's feast of affection. The boy wrapped his arms around Joe's neck and held on to the family member who had been away at war and had just returned.

Uncle Jacob beamed. "I know, the Army said Joe might have a problem if he returned to a home with kids."

Grandpop put his hand on Tucker's shoulder. "Might, Tucker … they said he *might* have a problem. But, we know Joe. We raised him from a puppy."

Gramma scratched Joe behind his ears. The dog was gentle with her, seeming to sense that her age would not permit excessive roughness, even if it was play. She cupped the dog's face with her hands to meet his eyes. "Joe was my body guard, my errand boy, my blanket on cold nights, and my babysitter. Tucker, when you were about four, you rode your tricycle up on South Main Street in front of the house. I sent Joe down the highway to fetch you home. He walked along on the traffic side of you while you peddled your tricycle next to the grass." She wrapped her arms around Joe's neck. "God brought Joe back to us. He wouldn't hurt his boy. Besides, Tucker, you're not a kid anymore. You have proven you're a man."

Christy jumped down from the crook of the tree. "I remember Joe. Welcome back to your family, soldier."

"That's right, his family." Tucker said as he laughed. "Freddie, come meet Joe. He's finally back from the war."

Tucker looked around at the crowded back yard. Family of all sizes and connections on the family tree were all over the lawn, with friends spilling down the streets behind the house. Aunts, uncles, cousins, and one G.I. Joe, the wonder dog of the U.S. Army, were all there laughing and enjoying the night. Tucker's mom and dad weren't in lawn chairs or sitting on a blanket; but they didn't have to be present for him to have a family. In fact, he had more family than most kids. Actually, he knew his family was complete before the war hero returned. He made peace with the idea of family in the last few days, but he really didn't know when it happened.

Now that Joe was here, he would have another boy to play ball with. Maybe, just maybe, he and Joe would play tug of war with the ropes of the hammock the next time Tucker decided to get out the fuselage for his P-51 Mustang Fighter and string it up in the sky.

Glossary

Pg.   8   <u>cringe</u> (whole body's reaction to fear, raised
                shoulders, tight, crinkled eyes, jaw and face)

Pg.   10   <u>heeled</u>, <u>lace</u>-up <u>oxford</u> <u>shoes</u>

Pg.   12   <u>the jig was up</u> (His secret was out. He was
                caught)

Pg.   13   <u>awry</u> (away from the appropriate or planned
                course)

Pg.   13   <u>appropriate</u> (suitable or fitting for a particular
                purpose)

Pg.   13   <u>dialing one long and four shorts on a party
                line</u> (A single phone line shared by several users
                Using crank on side of phone, caller would turn
                crank around one full revolution for a short ring
                and around two times for a long ring)

Pg.   14   <u>Lag Screw</u>

Pg.   20   <u>ja</u> (Pennsylvania Dutch meaning yes)

Pg.   20   <u>daresn't</u> (Pennsylvania Dutch meaning dare
                not = shouldn't)

Pg.   21   <u>clodhoppers</u>

Pg.   21   <u>Grandma Hooley Salve</u> (a drawing salve – pulls irritations from under the skin caused by splinters, thorns, bug bites, infection from wound)

Pg.   28   <u>transgression</u>   (violation of rule, a sin)

Pg.   30   <u>gut</u> (Pennsylvania Dutch meaning good)

Pg.   31   <u>mellow</u> (soft and rich sound)

Pg.   33   <u>dummkopf</u> (Pennsylvania Dutch/German meaning dumb idiot)

Pg.   35   <u>Interurban</u>   (a bus or other transportation between two cities)

Pg,   35   <u>stake</u> <u>truck</u>

Pg.   37   <u>gut</u>   (Pennsylvania Dutch meaning good)

Pg.   37   <u>wall</u> <u>hanging</u> <u>crank</u> <u>phone</u> (ebay)

Pg.   39   <u>jig</u>   (jig – a device to guide a woodworking piece in order to make an exact copy)

Pg.   43   <u>*conk*-*la*-*ree*</u> (the sound of the red-winged bird)

Pg.   48   <u>sentinel</u> (to stand and keep watch)

Pg.   50   <u>K-Rations</u> (WWII separate packages of concentrated or evaporated food)

　　　　　　　　　　　　　　

Pg.　　50　　pemmican biscuits (The earliest biscuit used for the "parachute ration" was a pemmican biscuit. This biscuit consisted of wheat, soybeans, corn, oats, dried skimmed milk, and beef muscle and liver compressed together with hydrogenated oil.)

Pg.　　50　　panorama (a wide, unblocked view of an area in all directions)

Pg.　　51　　saga (a long story with dramatic events)

Pg,　　52　　masquerade (dressed to pretend to be something or someone you are not)

Pg.　　52　　bogus (fake, not real, meant to trick the viewer)

Pg.　　54　　telephone switchboard (operator speaks to caller into the speaker around his/her neck, gets the name of the person to be called, and makes the connection by plugging it into the board - ebay)

Pg.　　59　　sanctuary (the room in a church with the alter, where people go to worship)

Pg.　　59　　pump organ (ebay)

Pg.　　64　　introit (the opening music of a church service played on organ or piano)

Pg.　　64　　adolescents (the period in life between childhood and adulthood)

Pg.   75   competitive (needing to compete or succeed and plan to win)

Pg.   75   agile (quick and well-coordinated)

Pg.   76   conscious (awake and aware of surroundings)

Pg.   76   concerto (a musical composition with at least two musical instruments)

Pg.   81   ice box (ebay)

Pg.   83   java (coffee beans first came from Java, Indonesia – the term java now refers to coffee)

Pg.   83   accomplishment (something done well)

Pg.   85   plain living (finding joy in simple things, being content with less)

Pg.   85   *The Lone Ranger* (a radio program first broadcast in 1933, then on television from1949 to 1957, created by George W. Trendle and developed by writer Fran Striker. Theme song was Gioachino Rossini's *William Tell Overture).*

Pg.   89   Maytag wringer-washing machine

Pg.   90   Philco radio

Pg.   91   <u>chassis</u> (frame to which the components are
                mounted)

Pg.   91   <u>mechanism</u> (a system of parts working together
                in a machine)

Pg.   98   <u>moseyed</u> (walk or move in a leisurely manner

Pg.   100   <u>root cellar</u> (a structure, usually dug underground
                or partially underground, used for storage of
                vegetables, fruits, nuts, and other foods)

Pg.   102   <u>das ist gut</u> (Pennsylvania Dutch meaning
                that/this is good)

Pg.   103   <u>momentum</u> (the quality of motion, or rhythm, of
                a moving body)

Pg.   103   <u>boogied</u> (dance to fast pop or rock music, or to
                move fast)

Pg.   104   <u>loss it</u> (Pennsylvania Dutch - "Ya daresn't loss
                it," means "you dare not lose it.")

Pg.   108   <u>drop-down toaster</u> (toast with drop-down sided)

Pg.   115   <u>diabolical</u> (evil, ungodly)

Pg.   121   <u>stifled</u> (to stop oneself from acting, like not
                letting yourself giggle)

Pg,   122   <u>air chuck</u>

Pg.   129   <u>scamp</u> (a person, especially a child, who is
                mischievous in a likable or amusing way)

Epilogue

Joe, a mixed breed German shepherd, did not return to the house on the corner after World War II. Bill (Tucker) remembers when Uncle Jule (Jacob) received Joe's Purple Heart and a letter explaining that children in the home may not be safe around discharged War Dogs. The dog with Bill in the picture above, was one of several pets that filled their home with joy and protection.

While he was still in school, Bill found a book in the library about World War-II War Dogs. The author described the heroic deeds of a dog, donated by a family to the war department for the Army's K-9 Corps. Bill still looks for a copy of the old book in every antique mall we visit.

● ● ● ● ●

Tucker McBride is both fact and fiction. Tucker is actually my husband Bill, so I heard the stories of his antics for many years. While he actually did the acts described, the timing is fictional. What Tucker packed into a few days around July 4, 1946, Bill actually lived over a year, about 1950.

The house and church on South Main Street really exists. Gramma and Grandpop Moyer (Perninnah and Albert Kime) reared their own five children there at the turn of the century. Then, their youngest daughter, Helen's four children called it home after she died.

Characters in the book:

Older brother Jack is Tim. Older sisters Beverly and Merry are Carolyn and Betsy. Tucker's friend, Christy is a composite character of Merry, some cousins, and Bill's friends. To those who know the family, watch for name changes of aunts and uncles, cousins and friends.

After Helen's death, their father, Edger Rapp, remarried. He and Juanita had a son, Edger Jr., called Joe by family and friends. When Juanita filed for divorce and moved with Joe to California, Edger married a third time. He and Laura had a son, Gary. After Edgar died, Gary, then age ten, moved in with Merry, her husband, Carl, and their three daughters. While Bill and his siblings didn't grow up with Joe and Gary, it has been a joy to get to know them as brothers.

● ● ● ● ●

The Dunlap Evangelical Church became the Dunlap EUB Church when the Evangelicals merged with the United Brethren in Christ Church on November 16, 1946. In 1968 the EUBs merged with the Methodists to become the United Methodist Church.

Grandma Dunn's Three Generation Nutmeg Sugar Cookies

Grandma Dunn was not really a Moyer relative. Mrs. Dunn was an older woman living in La Mesa, New Mexico, who gave me, the author, her family's three generation sugar cookie recipe many years ago when we lived there. She was very sweet and insisted I make the nutmeg tasting cookie dough exactly as she directed. Have fun following her unique way of making cookies. She said the recipe came from her great-grandmother, three generations back.

<u>Mrs. Dunn's Three Generation Sugar Cookies</u>

    2 cups flour on flour board
    1 cup slightly rounded Crisco in bowl
    1 cup sugar in same measuring cup as sugar to get all out
    Blend sugar and Crisco thoroughly
    1 egg beaten in separate bowl – add to sugar and Crisco
    1 cup buttermilk measured in same measuring cup as
            above ingredients and put into the small egg bowl
            to get
    out all the egg
    Add to 1 cup flour:
            1 kitchen teaspoon nutmeg
            1 kitchen teaspoon Clabber Girl baking powder
    Put ½ kitchen teaspoon soda into buttermilk
    Put 1 kitchen teaspoon lemon extract into sugar and
            Crisco
    Next: Add buttermilk and baking soda
            Add the cup flour with baking powder and nutmeg
            in it to Crisco and sugar etc.Mix thoroughly
            Add another 1 ¾ (little over) cup flour
            Add entire mixture to the 2 cups flour on the
            board
                    Mix and fold in all with hands – not all
                    the flour will fold in

       There will be plenty of flour left on board
Put dough back into bowl
Put small amount of dough on the floured board
and roll out thin – heavy paper thin
       Can be rolled out thicker – like a
       Christmas cookie – adjust the baking time
       Sprinkle with sugar
Cut out with cookie cutters or floured glass
Put on ungreased baking sheet touching edges
Press 1 raisin in center of each if you desire to
make as Mrs. Dunn taught
Makes 115 cookies if rolled out thin like above
Bake 425° for 8 minutes. With a thicker cookie
bake for 9 minutes

If you use raisins and sprinkle of sugar – plump
raisins by placing in water and boiling a few
minutes

SUMMER BEEF STICK

5 pounds hamburger (lean)
2½ teaspoons coarse ground pepper
4 Tablespoons Morton Tender Quick Curing Salt
2½ teaspoon Mustard Seed
2½ teaspoon Liquid Smoke
1 teaspoon to 3 teaspoons garlic powder (according to taste)

Directions: For 5 minutes per day knead like bread for 3 days (refrigerate between). On the 4th day, make 3 or 4 rolls and place on broiler pan. Grease will bake out.

Bake 9 hours in 160 degree oven.
Mrs. Nussbaum – Monroe, Indiana

TAPIOCA PUDDING

Recipe taken from Kraft Instant Tapioca box. Can follow their recipe. Re-printed below.

Shake box of dry tapioca before using

<u>Ingredients:</u>

1 egg
2 ¾ cups milk (use 2% or whole milk)
1/3 cup sugar
3 Tablespoons Kraft Minute tapioca
1 teaspoon vanilla
Directions: whisk egg and milk in a medium saucepan until blended. Stir in sugar and tapioca. Let stand 5 minutes. Bring to a full boil on medium heat, stirring constantly. Remove from heat. Stir in vanilla. Cool 20 minutes; stir. Can serve warm or chilled.

Make 6 servings - ½ cup each. For creamy pudding, press plastic wrap to surface as pudding cools.

Alternate Microwave Directions: Combine all ingredients except vanilla in large microwaveable bowl. Let stand 5 minutes. Microwave on high 10 – 12 minutes or until mixture comes to full boil, stirring every 3 minutes. Stir in vanilla.

NOODLES

2 ½ flour
1 pinch salt   (A pinch is about one-third of a fourth
teaspoon.)
2 eggs, beaten
½ cup milk
1 Tablespoon butter

Directions: In a large bowl, stir flour and salt. Add the beaten eggs, milk and melted butter. Knead the dough with your hands until smooth – 5 minutes. Cover bowl with a clean tea towel and let dough rest in bowl for 10 minutes.

Flour a surface - bread board, parchment paper, or other - roll out dough 1/8 to ¼ inch thick. Cut wide or narrow strips. Lay out strips on clean tea towels and allow to dry.

Cook: Add noodles to a large pot of boiling, salted water, cook to desired doneness, 10 – 20 minutes.

POTATO RIVEL SOUP

<u>To Begin</u>:

Wash, peel and chop 6 potatoes into large, bite size pieces. Put in large pan and cover with water. Boil potatoes until tender, about 20 minutes

<u>Rivels</u>

1 egg
1 cup flour
¼ teaspoon salt
Directions: Sift together flour and salt. Work 1 unbeaten egg into salted flour with hands. Mix until mixture looks like fine cornmeal. Set aside.

<u>Potato Soup</u>

6 Idaho or russet potatoes
½ cup butter
4 cups whole milk   (can use 2% but won't be as rich)
2 cups half and half   (for less rich use 2% milk)
1 teaspoon salt   (Gramma was on a low salt diet. Adjust to your needs)
¼ teaspoon pepper
1 teaspoon onion powder   (can used minced onion)
1 teaspoon garlic salt

<u>Directions</u>

In another large pan, over medium heat, melt butter. Slowly add milk and half and half, stir to blend
Stir in salt, pepper, onion powder and garlic salt. Stir in cooked potatoes

On medium heat, allow milk to bubble slightly around the edges of pot, about 5 – 20 minutes. Gradually drop rivel mixture loosely into potato soup, stir in lightly. Cover tightly and cook on low, 10 minutes. Serve in bowls.

Optional: Some may like grated cheddar or gouda cheese melted on top of their bowl of potato rivel soup.

APPLE SALAD – WALDORF SALAD

224

2 cups chopped apple - unpeeled
½ cup raisins
1 cup mini marshmallows
½ cup Miracle Whip
1 teaspoon lemon juice

Optional: one or more of the following may be added: ½ cup chopped celery, ½ cup walnuts or pecans, ½ - 1 cup sliced red grapes, chopped small banana, or ½ chopped pineapple

Mix together the Miracle Whip and lemon juice. Coat all ingredients with this mixture.

MUSH

1 ¼	cups cornmeal
2 ½	cups water
½	teaspoon salt

DIRECTIONS: Mix together cornmeal, water, and salt in a medium saucepan. Cook over medium heat stirring constantly, until mixture thickens. Takes about 5 – 7 minutes

If serving as cereal, put mush in bowls and add milk and sugar. If you want to fry it, pour the cooked mush into a loaf pan and chill over night or when completely chilled. Remove from pan, cut into slices ¼ to ½ inch thick depending on desired crispness. Fry in oil or melted butter over medium heat until brown on both sides. Serve hot with maple or other favorite syrup.

POTATO SALAD

6 medium to large potatoes – peeled, boiled, and diced
6 eggs – hard boil – chopped
1 cup sweet onion chopped
1 cup chopped celery
½ cup sweet pickle relish
Salt and pepper to taste – start with 1 teaspoon salt and add more
as needed to taste

> Dressing: 1 cup Miracle whip
> ¼ cup sugar
> 2 Tablespoons milk
> If tangy taste is desired, add a half teaspoon of
> yellow mustard and stir into dressing

Directions:

● Peel potatoes and chop into bite size pieces. In large pan, cover
with water and bring to boil. Boil until done – about 7-8 minutes
once water returns to boil. Test for doneness. Cool in refrigerator
with lid on.
● Boil eggs until hard boiled – about twenty-five minutes. Drain
and refrigerate in shell.
● In a large bowl: When eggs cool, peel, chop and add to cooled
potatoes. Add onion, celery, relish, and salt.
● Mix dressing, blending well and fold into potato mixture. If you
need more dressing, depending on size of potatoes, mix up more
dressing using the above proportions.
● Cover and put in refrigerator for several hours or overnight to
blend flavors.
● ENJOY

Other Books by Doris Gaines Rapp

Novels:
Escape from the Belfry
Escape from the Shadows
Murder, She Blogged – Just in Time Murder, She Blogged – Just in Time
(Fall 2019)
News at Eleven – A Novel
Length of Days – The Age of Silence (1ˢᵗ in the trilogy)
Length of Days – Beyond the Valley of the Keepers (2ⁿᵈ in the trilogy)
Length of Days – Search for Freedom
Hiawassee – Child of the Meadow
Smoke from Distant Fires

Children's Picture Book:
Shyloe and the Mayor
Lincoln's Christmas Mouse

Collection:
Christmas Feather, one of eight short stories by eight different authors in
a collection titled, *Christmases Past*

Non-Fiction:
Prayer Therapy of Jesus
Promote Yourself
Waiting for Jesus in a Can't Wait World – Advent 2014

Internet Presence
Facebook: Doris Gaines Rapp – Author Page
www.dorisgainesrapp.com
          www.dorisgainesrapp.blogspot.com
dorisgainesrapp@gmail.com
          www.prayertherapyrapp.blogspot.com

Watch for *Teacher's Guide to Tucker McBride* by Victoria Borgman. Discussion ideas, activities, writing prompts, and investigation ideas will be available on amazon.com and barnesandnoble.com. For information, go to www.dorisgainesrapp.com.

9 780998 859033